THE DESICCATED

PART ONE

N·J· EMBER

Published by Fire Lotus Books
Edited by Dionne Lister
Book cover design by Najla Qamber Designs
www.najlaqamberdesigns.com
Book design Inkstain Interior Book Design
www.inkstainformatting.com/

To anyone fighting their own battle,
you're stronger than you realize.
Keep going.

To Papa, thank you for being so understanding during every late
night. This book wouldn't have been possible without you.
To C.M. Deveraux, the best author the world never got a chance
to know. Thank you for all of the story notes, all of your
friendship and all of your love. I miss you, Twin.

THE
DESICCATED

PART ONE

CHAPTER ONE

OPHELIA THOMAS HAD been a liar for as long as she could remember. Everyone had lies they told themselves. Wasn't it only natural something born into a world of chaos would search for solace in the illusion of control? She did. Her routine, her town, her job, all fit neatly into predictable patterns shaped the way she lived. There was a rhythm to her days, the sounds and smells calming, like a familiar lullaby which helped her fall asleep at night. Sometimes, when not even the lies seemed enough to save her, she repeated them to herself like a prayer.

Black Ridge Falls is home. Black Ridge Falls is safe. I am in control. I am safe.

Growing up, her mom almost never read her fairytales, and in the rare times she did, she chose the originals full of darkness and gore. Classics like Shakespeare, Bronte and Austen were much more beloved because they portrayed a sort of truth in their tragedies. No one made it to happily ever after, and if they did, it was an uphill battle that earned you a few scars along the way. So it was no mystery why her mom had named her Ophelia, but with a name so full of death and insanity, it was also no mystery why she chose to go by Lia instead.

Right now, her mom reminded her of Briar Rose. Her strawberry blond hair fanned across her pillow, and her eyes were closed as if she were asleep. An IV was taped discreetly to the inside of her wrist while machines beeped quietly in the background. "What happened to you, Mom?"

It was the question she always asked. It was the question she couldn't *stop* asking, because no one had the answers. Lia pulled a chair up to her bedside and sat down, taking one of her mom's hands in her own. The hand didn't twitch or move, no matter how much she wished it would. Still, she held on.

Everyone called it a tragic accident. The best guess anyone had was somehow she must have slipped and fell, hitting her head on one of the kitchen counter's sharp edges. The injury caused swelling on her brain, and in order to save her life, the doctors induced a coma. There was always hope she would wake up, but as days turned into weeks, then months, then years, everyone moved on, leaving her mom hovering somewhere in the frail void between dreams and death.

"Ophelia Thomas?" A woman peered into the doorway, a clipboard in her hand.

"Lia," she corrected automatically. She swiped at a tear she hadn't known was there.

The woman smiled. "I'm Denise Farnsworth. I work in the billing department here. I don't mean to interrupt, but I had some concerns over the latest payment."

"What about it?" Lia tried not to sound irritated, but it seemed like everything set her on edge lately.

"I'm sorry to say, the last payment wouldn't go through. I was hoping to speak with the power of attorney." She consulted her clipboard. "Waylen Lancaster. Do you know who that is?"

Lia nodded. "He's my stepfather."

"Is he here today?"

"No, but I can give you his cell phone number."

"We already have a number for him. We've tried calling it several times over the last week." The woman rattled off a series of numbers. "Is that correct?"

Lia nodded again. "I can tell him to give you a call when he gets off work."

"Yes, thank you! That would help so much."

"Okay then." The pair stared at each other, unsure of what to say. The awkwardness stretched between them.

"Well, I'll let you get back to your visit. Thanks again." Denise Farnsworth gave Lia one last uncertain smile before she turned and left.

Checking the time on her cell, Lia saw she was late for work. "Next time I'll see if Lucy can come with me," she promised, giving her mom a quick kiss on the forehead. She picked her purse up off the floor and headed out. Her lime-green Converses slapped against the linoleum as she raced to catch one of the elevators before it closed. Missing it by just a few seconds, she anxiously tapped the down button as if the sheer force of her will would make it appear faster.

Eddie, her boss, wouldn't mind her being a few minutes late. She knew she was being ridiculous, but she couldn't help it. She watched the illuminated numbers climb to her floor. Six, seven, eight….The doors opened, and a piercing scream erupted out of the elevator. Lia jumped back, narrowly avoiding two exiting paramedics who were pushing a woman on a stretcher.

Lia couldn't look away from her. Delicate curls framed the pale woman's face. Blood poured out of her ears and nose, soaking the gauzy veil underneath her head and trickling down the delicate pearl beading on her dress. Streams of it leaked out of her eyes too and rolled down her cheeks like tears. "What's happening?" she wailed. "Why can't I see?"

The fear in the woman's voice made the hair on the back of her neck stand up. The thought of waking up one day without her sight made Lia shiver. A nurse ran towards them, and the paramedics slowed, blocking the entrance. Despite the urgency in her steps, her voice was calm, almost relaxed. Lifting each of the woman's eyelids, she shined a light into them. Pocketing it, she clucked her tongue. "Dr. Nettles is examining them in room six," she said. "It's down that hall there." She indicated the corridor to the left.

Lia stepped around them to push the down button again, her hip bumping the bed rail as she went past. Without warning, the woman's hand shot out and clamped down on her wrist. Lia winced, her instincts telling her to pull away from danger. "Hey! Let go."

Seeing her struggle, one of the ambulance attendants came around to help. He tugged at the woman's arm, but she tightened her grip. Her bloodshot eyes swiveled unseeingly in Lia's direction. "Please, just tell me….Did I make it out?"

"Ma'am you need to let go of her!"

"Did I make it out?!"

"Out of where?" Lia asked, trying to adopt the same calm the nurse had.

"Out of the quarantine. Willowpoint."

Lia's brow furrowed in confusion. "You're in Black Ridge Falls. I don't know what you're talking about."

The nurse filled a syringe full of something as the woman thrashed against her restraints. "Tell them to go back! They're killing us!"

"The fever's making her delirious," the nurse whispered to Lia. She held down the arm holding Lia's wrist and jabbed the syringe into her skin.

The effect was almost immediate. The woman's grip loosened,

her hand falling away as she sobbed quietly. "I don't want to die. They all died."

Lia's breath caught. "You're going to be fine," she said. It wasn't so much because she believed it, but, because, what else could you say? She was a liar, but she wasn't cruel. The woman's eyelids fluttered, and Lia escaped into the empty elevator. The woman slowly disappeared from view as the doors slid closed. Her weary voice called out just before it shut completely. "Please, don't let me die."

LIA'S HEART WAS still pounding as she drove to work. Sun glinted off the truck's hood, red dirt billowing up like clouds around her, but all she could see was the woman's bloody, red eyes and hear the terror in her voice. She clicked on the air conditioning, hoping the cold would calm her nerves and clear her head. Sweat made her legs stick to the seat. The heat was so high that summer you'd have thought Black Ridge Falls had an infection Mother Nature was determined to sweat out. Doctors warned residents to be careful of heatstroke and to stay indoors as much as possible, which is why she drove instead of walking to work like she usually did. The truck belonged to her best friend, E.J., but he let her borrow it whenever she needed. She slowed when she spotted the sign above all the other businesses around it: *Eddie's Overboard Grill.* The heat made the building look like it was shimmering in and out of focus, its terracotta and off-white exterior running together like paint on a wet canvas.

Overboard (as it was known by the town's residents) never had a problem attracting business, and despite the warnings, she could see a line already forming outside. As she walked towards the entrance, the usual mix of locals waved to her. There were also many road-weary tourists, most likely here for the annual strawberry festival. A pungent odor of sweat and perfume wafted along the interior as people crowded into the doorway, jostling her left and right as she fought her way inside.

"Lia!" E.J. shouldered in to grab her arm and guide her though the chaos. "I guess the food stalls aren't selling as well this year. We have more people here than they do at the fairgrounds."

She nodded, not trusting herself to speak. The restaurant's tangerine walls and gleaming wood furniture normally made it seem open and inviting, but that was fading fast as more and more people flooded inside to get respite from the scorching heat. E.J. said something to her, and she must have answered because he let go of her arm, and she auto-piloted her way to the kitchen, gathering empty plates and cups as she went.

It was twice as busy in back, than out front, and nobody paid attention to her as she dumped the dishes into an already cluttered bin. A soft hum droned in her ears, and her heart raced. She wiped her damp palms on the front of her apron before reaching behind herself to clutch the edge of the sink. Drawing in deep, shaky breaths, Lia shut her eyes and tried to block out all the noise. *Calm down*, she thought. *Pull yourself together.* It was almost two years since her last anxiety attack, but she hadn't missed them.

"Are you okay, mija?"

Her boss, Eddie, was standing over her. Somehow she had ended up crouched in a ball on the floor. "Fine," she told him.

"You don't look fine. Maybe you should take a break."

Her eyes widened. "You're kidding, right? We're already short on people."

"Yeah, because two of my waitresses collapsed at work and

ended up in the hospital. I don't want you being number three. Go on."

She wanted to argue, but part of her was glad for the excuse to stop and collect herself. She meant to go into the bathroom, but her nerves got the better of her, and she sank into one of the empty booths with her back to the window. She drew her legs up and rested her head on her knees. *Maybe I should go home.*

After a few minutes of deep breathing, the knot in her chest loosened and the numbness in her limbs faded. When she finally looked up, she saw the only other waitress was struggling to keep up with her tables. Feeling guilty, she sprang to her feet and pushed through the crowd. Bumping into the backs of chairs and squeezing past customers, she was nearly out of breath by the time she reached for the two plates sitting in the order window.

"Lia!" Eddie called in warning.

"I'm okay!" She yelled back. "And Amy's getting crushed out here."

She weaved her way to a waiting table, set the food down with an apologetic smile to the family sitting there and moved on to a couple who was waiting to place their order.

"Sorry about that," she said. Even though the guy with his

thick brown hair, toned muscles and scowl looked a little intimidating, it was the girl who made her uneasy. Lia couldn't figure out why. Her hair was platinum with bubble-gum-pink streaks, shaved up the back into some kind of asymmetrical bob. She wore a pair of patchwork overalls over a floral crop top, and her eyes were covered by mirrored aviator sunglasses. Maybe it was the aggressive vibe they projected; she could see it in the tension in his shoulders and the attitude in her lifted chin. She gave them a strained smile and poised her pen on the pad. "Can I start you off with something to drink?"

The guy spoke first. "Is your tea made with tap water?"

Lia tried not to roll her eyes. She hated the nitpicky ones. "Yes, it is."

"What about your lemonade?" the girl asked.

"Yes, our lemonade is also made from tap water." Lia caught Amy's eye as she was giving menus to another table. The other waitress shook her head.

"Anything that isn't?"

Lia turned her attention back to the girl and was jarred to see her face reflected off the aviator glasses. "The pop comes from the machine."

"Then we'll take two pops," the guy said.

Lia went to get them. When the time came for their food orders, she braced herself for another round of questions, but that didn't happen. The pair ordered without any special requests and thanked her when she went to fill their order. Eventually one of the new hires came in for her shift and took over, giving Lia the opportunity to take a real break. She grabbed some half-melted pitchers of sweet tea and lemonade off a few tables, slide sideways through the kitchen doors and let out a sigh of relief as they swung shut behind her. Sweat had pooled at the base of her neck, making the robin's-egg-blue work shirt cling to her. The air felt dry and thick, pressing her on all sides like a rapidly deflating balloon.

"You honestly don't pay me enough for this, Eddie," she said. "Do you have the thermostat set to slow-roast or what?"

Eddie glanced up from the grill and pointed a spatula at her. "The way you move, Ophelia, you're lucky I'm paying you at all."

She rolled her eyes and smiled. Good. The banter was back. Hopefully, he had forgotten her mini-breakdown from earlier. Lia tipped the slush from the pitchers into the sink, rinsed them out and refilled them with fresh tea from the fridge. When she turned around, she noticed the other cooks watching her out of their peripheral vision. Okay, so maybe not everyone had forgotten it.

She was on her way out when Amy poked her head through the order window. "Hey, Lia? A neighbor's here with your little sister. She's asking for you."

Lia frowned. "What? Lucy's supposed to be with her dad today."

Amy raised her hands in a helpless "don't ask me" gesture. Lia followed her.

"Sissy!" the five year old shouted as soon as she saw Lia. Mrs. Ryan from across the street gave Lia an apologetic look as Lucy sprinted through the crowd. She caught Lucy mid-run and scooped her into her arms. She was wearing the same overalls Lia had helped her dress in for school this morning, her strawberry blond curls half falling out of the elastic tie that kept it out of her face. Lia smoothed it away from her sweaty forehead.

"Hey, ladybug," said Lia. "I thought you were spending the day with daddy."

"I tried to get off the bus when it brought me home, but the driver wouldn't let me."

By now Mrs. Ryan had made her way to them. "Lia, dear,

how are you?"

"I'm just fine Mrs. Ryan. Thank you for looking after Lucy. I guess Waylen forgot I had to work."

"It's no trouble at all. I would've kept her until someone came home, but I have a client meeting in Willowpoint in about an hour. I tried calling your father, but it went to voicemail."

"*Stepfather*," Lia corrected with a thin smile. "Don't worry about it, Mrs. Ryan."

Something she said bothered Lia; some question was right there at the tip of her tongue, but she couldn't pinpoint what it was. While she was thinking, Mrs. Ryan was already pushing past customers to the exit. Lucy looked at Lia.

"I guess you're spending the day at work with me, ladybug."

Lucy raised a tiny fist in triumph, and Lia laughed. She put her down and guided her to a booth. Lucy climbed in, scooted all the way to the window and dropped her backpack on the bench beside her. E.J. hurried over to clear off the table. "Hey, kid." He ruffled her hair.

"I get to spend the day with Sissy."

E.J. held up his palm, and they high fived. Once Lia had given Lucy a placemat and crayons, she went back to her tables.

About an hour later, E.J. pulled her aside. "Hey, are you feeling okay?" he asked.

"Yeah, I'm fine."

"You sure? Dad said you had a fit or something earlier."

E.J. was Eddie's son and had been working at Overboard ever since he was old enough. Lia couldn't remember his mom very well. She had gotten sick when they were very young. Lia's memories of her were hazy at best. Still, memories of her illness had stuck with E.J., and he got antsy anytime someone was ill. He'd been even more worried since two of the waitresses were taken away in an ambulance last week. Lia could imagine how he must have reacted when he heard about her panic attack. She put a hand on his shoulder. "I was a little stressed out, but I'm fine. Promise."

Relief crossed his face. E.J. opened his mouth to say something, but a loud thud sounded, halting him. More followed, creating a frantic drumbeat from above. The noise grew so loud it muffled the screams from a woman in the front of the restaurant. Chills ran up the back of Lia's neck. What was out there?

People stood and pointed towards the large front window. Lia thought of Lucy and ran. She almost tripped on a chair leg and grabbed the back of a booth to catch herself. She reached out to her sister, who had her face pressed up against the glass. She protested when Lia gripped her in a hug. "Look!" she said, pointing up.

Lia stared outside before jumping back. Tiny brown masses fell from the sky. As they hurtled towards the ground, Lia realized what they were. Sparrows. Hundreds of them. Maybe thousands. One collided with the window and left a sticky red trail as its body slid down the length of it.

Its glassy black eyes stared back at her, lifeless.

CHAPTER
TWO

TEARING HER GAZE away, Lia crawled backwards out of the booth, taking her sister with her. People crowded around them, all of whom were looking as if they wanted to run but had decided against it when they realized what they'd be running towards. Lia looked down at Lucy, who was still staring at the falling sparrows in wonder, and then scanned the room to find Eddie. Her gaze landed on the picky couple from earlier. Everyone in the restaurant who wasn't clamoring to get a better look at what was going on was fighting their way to the nearest exit. But not them. They were silently finishing their meal as if they had all the time in the world. The man looked up and locked eyes with Lia, which flustered her. She focused on her sister instead. "Lucy, I want you to stay here while I go find Eddie, okay? Stay right here."

She made her way to Eddie's office, which was past the kitchen and up the staircase near the back exit. He was seated behind his desk with a telephone to his ear. "Uh huh. Well, I don't know how easy that's going to be, Otis…" Seeing her, Eddie motioned for her to come inside, and she dropped into the chair across from him. "We'll do the best we can, but we do have a packed house. I'd appreciate it if you could send some folks sooner rather than later." He paused to listen. "Okay then, bye." He hung up.

"Was that Sheriff Manning?" Lia asked.

Eddie nodded. "He wants us to keep everyone from leaving until he can get some people over here, but it could be a while."

"Why?"

"Apparently this happened all over town. They're still trying to organize cleanup crews to get rid of all of it."

"Unreal."

"That's one word for it. Anyway, I'll need you and the others to help me keep an eye on things until they get here. I'll be down in a minute to explain everything to the customers."

She didn't think this was going to go well but headed downstairs anyway. When she reached the bottom step, she nearly collided with the picky couple from earlier. "Sorry," said the guy, who reached out his hands to steady her.

"What are you doing back here?" Lia demanded.

"Well...I didn't catch your name?" He gave her one of those ear-to-ear grins E.J. always used to talk his way out of something.

She narrowed her eyes. "Lia."

"It's nice to meet you, Lia."

"Save it. I've caught you doing... I don't know what, but you need to go back into the dining room where everyone else is. You and...." It was then Lia noticed the girl he had been with had disappeared.

She turned back to him. He shoved past her, knocking her to the ground as he made a run for the back door. A sharp pain shot up her hip and her vision blurred. By the time she had recovered enough to be infuriated and go after them, she heard an engine roaring out of the parking lot.

"What happened?" asked Eddie, helping her up yet again

from the floor.

"I honestly don't know."

"DON'T YOU THINK it's weird?" Lia asked E.J. as he drove her and Lucy home later. Eddie had closed for the day after the officers from the sheriff's department came and took everyone's statements. She gave a description of the couple so they could be questioned if they needed to, but she hadn't mentioned them to anyone else.

"Weird, sure. I don't think it's anything for people to be worked up about," he said. "So some birds fell from the sky. It happens."

"They fell all over town. At the same time," she insisted. "Something feels off about it."

"Just because they haven't found an explanation, doesn't mean there isn't one." E.J. wiped sweat from his brow and turned down the road toward her house. He looked flushed, and his hands tightened on the wheel.

"Are you okay?" Lia asked.

"Yeah, I'm fine. It's the heat."

She raised the knob on the air conditioner and turned one of the vents in his direction. "Promise me you'll stay in the rest of the night. You were in the sun a really long time helping those guys clear the birds off the lot. You need to keep cool."

E.J. made a face. "Yes, Mom." He glanced at her. "How is your mom? You went to see her today, didn't you?"

Lia nodded. "She's the same. I don't know why I keep expecting it to be any different."

"It isn't wrong to have hope, Lia."

Lia shrugged. She didn't mention she hadn't felt anything like hope in almost two years. For so long her life revolved around one purpose: take care of Lucy and make sure she was happy. It was overwhelming in the beginning. Waylen was gone, and she had never had to be any kind of parental figure before. Just the thought of how many ways she could screw up used to trigger a panic attack. But then Eddie stepped in, letting them stay with him and E.J. and working with her to make a schedule that allowed her time to take care of her little sister while still having time for herself. Living there showed Lia what it meant to be a family, for better and worse.

Then Waylen came back....

"Lia?"

"What?"

"We're here."

She looked out the passenger window to see her familiar run-down country-styled house. She frowned at the shaggy grass scorched brown from the heat, and the shriveled tulips slumped over dejectedly under the front window. At least she had something to keep her busy on her day off tomorrow. The mailbox was full, and her stepfather's car wasn't in the driveway. She climbed out and unbuckled a sleeping Lucy from her car seat, lifting her up so she could carry her. Reaching inside for her purse, she threw it over her left shoulder and shut the door. "Thanks for the ride."

The path leading to the porch was cracked and uneven, and Lia took her time so she wouldn't trip. The screen door squeaked as she pushed it open, and just as she unlocked the interior door, the phone rang from inside. The wooden door always stuck in the summer months, and she cursed as she struggled to push it open.

When it finally swung free, Lia laid her sister on the couch and threw her purse into an armchair. Sprinting to the kitchen, she answered the phone just as the machine picked up. "Hello?"

"Hello, is this Lia?"

"Uh huh. I mean, yes, this is Lia."

"Hi, Lia, this George Ryan. I'm sorry to bother you, but I was wondering if you've talked to my wife today."

"I talked to her earlier when she brought Lucy to Overboard. She said she had a meeting in Willowpoint."

"And that was the last time you spoke to her?"

"Yeah. Is everything okay, Mr. Ryan?"

"Probably. It's just I haven't talked to her since after she left Overboard, and she usually checks in by now."

"Maybe her phone died on the way back?"

"You're probably right, but would you mind giving me a call if you hear from her?"

"Of course. Have a good night, Mr. Ryan."

"You too."

Lia returned the phone to the base and went to lock the door. Once the door was locked, she kicked off her shoes. It wasn't the greatest idea to let Lucy keep sleeping because she would probably be wide awake all night, but the idea of an uninterrupted shower was too good to pass up. As she slid down the hall in her socked feet, she couldn't help but glance at the faded squares on the wall where the family photos used to hang. After her mom's accident, Waylen made her take all of them down because he said seeing her in them was too painful. After eight months of the three of them living together, there were barely any traces of her mom left in the house. To Lia, it was almost as if he wanted it to seem like her mom had never existed at all.

Her room was at the end of the hall on the left. The walls were white, with a dark oak dresser and a twin bed tucked against the window. Most of what she had was still packed away in plastic tubs labeled with her mom's messy scrawl. She had stacked them in a corner of her room by the closet, and each time she looked at them, her stomach dropped in embarrassment. When Lia had come back home, it hadn't been to stay it had only been to visit and patch things up with her mom. It was Christmas, just after she had finished her sophomore year in college. All the lights had been on, the front door open. She hadn't thought anything of it until she walked into the kitchen and saw blood everywhere and her mom unconscious on the floor. She would never forget Lucy's wails drifting from her room at the end of the hallway. Even though the sheriff's office had investigated, no one had any idea where Waylen had gone.

The situation had left Lia with a choice: drop out of college and take care of her sister or leave her to the state, where she would most likely never see her again. Lia had never doubted what must be done. She called the school and withdrew from classes. Lucy was only three at the time, and Lia didn't have any parenting experience so Eddie offered to let them stay at his house and help Lia look after her sister. She had thought about staying in their house instead, but every time she walked past the kitchen, she couldn't help seeing what had happened.

They had been living at Eddie's for a year when Waylen showed up during Thanksgiving, demanding Lucy be returned to him. Waylen wouldn't tell her where he had been or why and Lia wasn't going to leave her sister with him, so they agreed Lia would move back into the house and help Waylen take care of Lucy.

The new, unfamiliar, happier version of Lia drifted further away---her life at college a distant memory and all the problems she tried to leave behind were seeping back in---she began to feel helpless, then hopeless, and now... Lia was drowning, and she didn't know how to fight her way out. New Lia was gone, but she wasn't ready to say goodbye to her. It felt like admitting she had failed.

She yanked the lid off a bin that held most of her clothes and retrieved one of her pajama sets. Even though it was sweltering outside, she grabbed a set with pants instead of shorts. She rolled everything up and carried it to the bathroom. Of all the places in the house, the bathroom reminded her of her mom the most. Before her mom had met Waylen, Lia and her parents lived in California. Even though her mom didn't like talking about her life with Lia's father, the memories of the ocean were the one thing she held onto. There were tiny white seashells decorating the sandy beige wallpaper, and the shower curtain had a mermaid on it.

Lia showered and dressed quickly, happy to be free of the sweat and grime from working all day. She woke Lucy and wandered into the kitchen to see what she could make for dinner. The kitchen was connected to the dining room and showed signs of being well lived in. Sage-green paint covered the walls and contrasted sharply with the deep-brown baseboards. The white-granite counter tops had a few small cracks, and the appliances were sparse. White, patterned linoleum covered the floor until it met with the dark hardwood of the living room and hallway. It was still stained in the corner where her mother had fallen, and each time she entered the room, it took her everything she had not to stare at it.

Opening the refrigerator, Lia could see tonight would be a rummage dinner, where she pulled something together from whatever she could find. All that was left was a wilted head of lettuce, a few tomatoes, an almost empty container of orange juice and a pound of ground hamburger. She pulled out the hamburger and opened the cupboards, shuffling things around until she found a box of macaroni and cheese hidden in the back. "Hey, lady bug, how does hamburger mac sound for dinner?"

"With ketchup?" Lucy asked.

Lia wrinkled her face in disgust. She thought they would be through with the ketchup-on-everything phase by now. Realizing it was probably the only way she would get her sister to eat tonight, she sighed. 'With ketchup," she said and reached down to get a frying pan. While she waited for the meat to brown and the pasta to boil, Lia gathered all of her trash and carried it to the trashcan. She stomped on the pedal to lift the lid, and just before she threw everything in, a crumpled piece of bright-orange paper caught her eye. It was the only thing in the otherwise empty bag. She grabbed it, setting it aside as she threw everything else away. After she had washed her hands, drained the water from the macaroni and stirred in the cheese sauce, Lia picked it up again, smoothing it out on the kitchen table and praying she was wrong.

She wasn't. The orange paper was something everyone in the neighborhood had come to associate with notices from the landlord, and Lia had never heard of it bearing good news. This was a letter from their landlord to Waylen, telling him if he didn't come up with rent money soon, he was going to evict them.

Lia struggled to breathe, feeling like she had been kicked in the stomach. This couldn't happen. What were they going to do? And why would Waylen not saying anything about it?

Lucy walked into the kitchen and climbed into her usual chair at the table. "Is dinner ready yet?"

Lia frantically folded up the letter and slipped it into her pocket. "Yeah, just a second." She mixed the food together and ladled it into one of Lucy's cartoon bowls. She made another one for herself and poured them both the last of the orange juice. After she set it down, Lucy looked up at her. "Ketchup, please, Sissy?"

On her way back to the refrigerator, headlights flashed through the kitchen curtains. Good. If Waylen was home, they could talk about what was going on. Lia drizzled the ketchup onto her sister's pasta and sat down to wait for him to come in. She heard the screen door open and then slam shut. Thinking he left his toolbox in the car again, Lia picked up her fork and started to eat. She sat it down when the lights flashed again and she heard an engine backing out of the driveway. "Stay here, Lucy."

Lia went to the front door, opened it and stepped onto the porch. There were no streetlights in Black Ridge Falls. When night fell, it was hard to see anything at all, so she nearly missed the note taped there. Lia ripped it off and brought it inside. The handwriting wasn't from anyone she recognized, and it was printed on a piece of torn stationary from the Seabreeze Motel. As she read it, a nauseating current of dread flooded her stomach.

"Whatever you do, don't drink the water."

CHAPTER THREE

WHEN LIA WOKE the next morning, the first thing she saw was the cornflower-blue eyes of Lucy. She was curled up on her side, tucked in close and watching Lia with a tiny smile on her face. A rush of warm affection filled her heart. It was hard to explain, but there were certain times when it hit Lia just how much she loved her little sister, and she realized she would do anything to protect her. She felt it must've been very similar to the fierce emotion a mother has for her child.

Lia lifted her head off her pillow to check the light outside her bedroom window. The dim glow told Lia the sun was barely up. She lowered her head and fixed Lucy with a look that was meant to be stern, but she knew it wasn't. "What are you doing up, little miss?"

Lucy giggled.

Lia brushed hair away from her face. "Do you want to sleep in here?"

She'd been climbing into Lia's bed more and more, even when she fell asleep in her own bed first. Lucy nodded, sucking her thumb, and Lia yanked the thin sheet up and over so it covered them. It didn't matter how warm it was, both girls refused to sleep without something covering them. Her sister wiggled around until she was facing away from her. Lia protectively draped an arm over her. Lucy placed one of her hands over Lia's arm, as if to make sure she wasn't going anywhere. This was new, strange behavior and it worried Lia. "What is it, buggy? What's the matter?" Her sister snuggled closer.

After, Lia found herself unable to get back to sleep. Maybe seeing the birds falling yesterday gave her nightmares? That would make sense. Guilt washed over her. She should have been with Lucy the whole time.

From where she lay, she could see the stack of bins in the corner. She stared at them for awhile, willing her body to drift back to sleep, but it wouldn't. The light in her room grew brighter, and the sound of dishes being moved around came from the kitchen. Lia rose, checked to make sure Lucy was still covered and followed the sound.

Waylen stood by the counter, sipping from a travel thermos. His eyes were the same cornflower-blue as her sister's. But they were red-rimmed and bloodshot, like he hadn't slept in awhile. He was dressed for work. His rumpled t-shirt and frayed jeans were the kind of clothes he didn't mind getting ruined by splattered paint or ripped by stray nails. Lia brushed past him as she went to fill her own mug with coffee and flinched. Lia took a few steps to widen the space between them and gently lifted things on and off the counter so she wouldn't make noise.

You don't need to do that anymore, she told herself. *Waylen is better now.* Was that one of his lies? Or one of her own? Lia watched his hands out of the corner of her eye. The tremors were there, almost imperceptible, but she knew how to look for the signs better than anyone. Adding in the fact he was staying out all night again.... She didn't like what that said.

"Lia?" Waylen put his hand on her shoulder. She jumped like she had been electrocuted. The hand on her coffee cup jerked, sloshing the contents all over the counter. Scalding liquid splattered her pajama top. Her eyes welled up against the shock.

I need to get out of here.

"Jesus, are you okay?" He grabbed her arm and turned on the tap, thrusting her arm under the cool water. She hadn't even felt her arm burn.

"Fine," she choked out. "I'm fine." She wrenched her arm out of his grip and cradled it to her chest. "Did you need something?"

"I asked if everything went okay yesterday. I realized when I got in last night I was supposed to watch Lucy."

"Mrs. Ryan brought her up to work after school. E.J. gave us a ride after. Crisis averted."

Waylen nodded and then pointed to the spilled coffee. "You going to clean that up?"

Lia flushed with embarrassment. "Sorry." *Stupid. He shouldn't have to tell me what to do. It should already be done.* She tore some paper towel off of the roll and wet it, wiping down her cup fist and then the counter. "Where were you yesterday, anyway?"

He refilled his thermos. "I got called into work." He wouldn't look at her. "You're off today, right?"

"Yeah… yes. I need to get groceries first. Is it okay if I go now? I just need to change."

"Fine. Don't take too long. I'm getting picked up at ten."

Lia checked the clock. It was just after eight. "I'll definitely be back by then."

She paused before leaving the kitchen. "Our rent payment's already handled for this month, right?"

Waylen was already busy looking at the paper. "Yeah, all taken care of."

THE TRICK TO telling a believable lie is to believe in it so much you forget it's a lie to begin with. Waylen lied to her. If she didn't know any better, didn't know him, would she be able to tell it wasn't the truth?

Lia climbed into his car, the back filled with groceries, and checked the time on the dashboard. Just because he wouldn't tell her the truth didn't mean she was out of people to ask. Taking a deep breath, she started the engine.

The Clover was an after-work staple for Waylen and his

work buddies, and as she walked from the acrid heat outside to the cool interior of the bar, Lia saw more than a few familiar faces nursing a drink. They nodded to her in greeting, and she gave them with a shy wave. She didn't drink often and the one time she had really let loose ended with disastrous results, so while she waited, she ordered a club soda instead. Just as she was about to give up on the whole idea, she noticed her landlord slip in and sit in a booth across the room. She waited until he was busy giving his order to the waitress before she approached him. "Hey, Lance," she said.

His smile looked forced, and it confirmed her fears. "Lia."

"I can fix this."

Lance didn't ask her what she was talking about. They both knew.

He looked away. "I'm sorry, kid. It isn't personal. I have to make a living like everyone else."

She took the seat across from him and glared. "And I have a five year old sister at home who has gotten used to having a place to sleep at night."

"C'mon, don't do that." The waitress arrived with his scotch and he took a hearty swig from the glass before she could set it on the table.

Lia didn't let up. "Then don't throw us out. Give me a week to come up with what we owe." She wasn't sure how she would do it, but she knew she would. She had to.

"You couldn't afford it." His face was grim. "And even if you could, Waylen would just wind up short again next month."

"What do you mean?"

"Your step-dad's got a gambling problem," he whispered. "If you don't believe me, go over there and ask some of those guys when the last time was he came to work."

The more she thought about it, the more everything started making sense. The money withdrawals, the staying out until early hours of the morning and the gifts he brought home, even though they were already strapped for cash. The next thing Lance said made her blood run cold. "Plus, the guy's a complete sociopath. You know that, right? You should, considering all the things he used to do to your mom."

Lia's mouth went dry, and she sipped a little of her pop. There it was: their family secret. The one her mom told her to never talk about to anyone. Yet somehow, it seemed like Lance already knew.

"Yes," she answered, whispering. Her fingers trembled, shaking the glass. She set it down on the tabletop and placed her hands in her lap, clasping them together.

His gaze softened into something. *It better not be pity*, she thought.

"Why don't you go back to college? Leave your mom and Waylen's problems for them to figure out."

"I won't leave her." She realized it might have been unclear about whom she meant. "Lucy."

"That's not your responsibility."

Lia squeezed her eyes shut at the anger rushed through her when people said that. They didn't know. They couldn't understand. She reached up to tug on a key charm dangling from her necklace. "She's just a little girl. If I leave, she'll have no one. She deserves to have someone who will fight for her. She deserves to know she matters enough to be fought for."

Lance took another swig of scotch, scribbled something on the napkin in front of him and folded it. "One week, and only because of you and your sister."

When she reached for it, Lance held onto it and didn't let go until she looked up at him. "You can't take on everything by yourself. Think about getting some help."

Far from being comforted, shame burned in her stomach and behind her eyes. How did she let it get this bad? How could she find help for something her mom couldn't find help for? "Okay."

LIA COULD FEEL the shadow of change creeping up behind her. There was a part of her knew, logically, she couldn't keep everything under her control, but if there was one person she was good at lying to, it was herself. She breathed deep and cleared her throat, pushing down the emotions threatening to break open and suffocate her from the inside. She gripped the steering wheel as tears blurred her vision. *I will not be weak. I will not be weak.* Except she was, and she hated it.

The self-loathing turned into sobs, and she pulled over to the side of the road. Fishing tissues out of the glove box, she wiped her tears and blew her nose. "I can do this. I'll figure it out."

A loud knock on the driver's side window made her jump.

A woman stood there. Framed by brown curly hair, hazel eyes stared at Lia, the green flecks within them standing out against the woman's many freckles. Lia rolled her window. "Hey, Anita." She was ghostly pale and a sheen of sweat covered her face and neck. It reminded Lia of the woman from the hospital. "Are you okay?"

Anita opened her mouth and coughed. Blood sprayed Lia's face and the window. Frozen with shock, Lia watched as she made wet gurgling sounds and more blood ran over her lips and down her chin.

"Oh shit," Lia whispered. Snapping out of it, she rooted around in her purse for her phone. "Hang on, Anita, I'm going to call for help."

The call finally connected. "Hello, what's your emergency?"

"Hi, I need an ambulance. There's a woman vomiting blood and—"

An arm reached in and unlocked the door. A man grabbed her, knocking the phone out of her hand and onto the floor. "Help!" She screamed and kicked, struggling until he punched her in the stomach and dropped her on the road. *I don't understand. What's happening?* Pain stabbed at her stomach.

Fighting for breath, Lia was now eye to eye with Anita. Her breathing was also labored, and her eyes were wild, as if she didn't understand where she was. The woman grabbed Lia's arm and she yelped. *Not again*, she thought as the pressure increased. Pain like a thousand needle pricks sliced into her skin. The inhuman wail of the other woman drowned out Lia's scream. Lia stared at her weakly.

Anita's back arched off the ground, her feet drawn into points in the dirt. Lia heard crunching as her spine broke free of her skin, and blood gushed out of the openings. Terrified, Lia yanked her arm away... the woman's hand dislocated from her wrist with a sickening pop. With her arm free, Lia rolled onto her back and cradled it to her chest.

Anita's eyes rolled up into her head leaving only the white visible. She stumbled to her feet and ran. As she zigzagged across the road, a van drove past her. She waved her undamaged arm over her head until she heard the engine shut off. When she opened her eyes a dark SUV sat inches from her. She stumbled through the mud to the side door.

"Help!" she shouted through the closed passenger window. "She's having some kind of fit."

The driver's door opened, and a man in a dark suit stepped out. Lia opened her mouth to speak until she realized he was reaching for a gun tucked into his waistband. Lia dropped to the ground. A shot rang out. Lia moved, staying low until she had cleared the side of the van. She straightened up and ran. She heard the van's sliding door and tried to run faster. *Where had the first man gone?* She yelled as someone grabbed her around the middle and lifted her off the ground. Lia screamed and struggled as they carried her back to van. Lia could see Anita's bloodied body as her line of sight cleared the hood of the vehicle. She wasn't moving.

The man holding her was trying to shove Lia through the open door, and she gripped the roof to try to stop him. The one who had at shot Anita was climbing past the driver's seat, slowly making his way back to them. He was confident, Lia realized--- neither of them expected her to get away.

Lia wasn't very strong, but running had made her leg muscles powerful enough for what she needed to do. As the one inside the van reached for her feet, she kicked with all her strength. Her shoe connected with something solid and she glimpsed the man clutching his nose before she toppled backward into the dirt, the momentum of her kick knocking the first one off balance.

Lia didn't waste any time; she ran as fast as she could down the road, weaving side to side to make herself a more difficult target. She didn't bother trying to see if they were following her. Chances were that if they weren't already, they soon would be. As she willed her legs to go faster, her calf muscles burning, another van came into view. Her heart kicked double time in her chest, and stupidly, she froze. This van was a lighter color than the other one, and she couldn't see who was driving, but she wasn't taking any chances. As the headlights illuminated her, she sprinted past the van as fast as she could.

It stopped. Someone yelled out the window, "Lia!"

The voice sounded familiar, but she couldn't place it with anyone she knew. Curiosity and exhaustion won over fear, and she doubled back. A vehicle would be a faster getaway than being on foot. She moved cautiously as she approached the driver side window. At the wheel sat a brunette man, about her age. She blanked on a name, but a memory of yesterday's shift came to her: this was one of her customers, the one who had pushed her. Instead of anger, relief coursed through her. "Nick."

"Get in."

Lia hesitated. She didn't know him. *What if he's involved?* The dark SUV was getting closer in the rearview mirror. A shot rang out. One of the back windows shattered. Out of options, Lia jumped inside and slammed the door. "Drive!" she yelled at the same time Nick yelled, "Get down!"

The engine roared as Nick slammed his foot down on the gas pedal. Lia scrambled to buckle her seatbelt as the acceleration forced her back into the seat. "Hold on," he said grimly. The trees smeared across her vision and she clawed at the seatbelt strap like it could somehow cause the van to slow and bring the world back into focus. She shut her eyes and prayed she wouldn't throw up. "Nick?"

"I've almost shaken them. Just hold on a couple more minutes." As promised, after a few minutes the van decelerated and Lia chanced opening her eyes. Nick was watching her out of the corner of his eye. "Do you know why they're after you?"

"Why would they be after me? Who were those guys?"

Nick didn't say anything. Lia stared him down. "If you know something, you're going to tell me right now. If my life is in danger...."

"Everyone's life is in danger."

"What does that mean?" When he didn't answer, Lia punched him in the arm. "Tell me what you're talking about!"

He huffed. "Just…don't drink the water, okay?"

"You were the one who left the note on my door?"

"Maybe."

Lia considered the new information. "Where are we going, anyway?"

"Where were you going before all of this happened?"

"Home." Lia went to check the time on her phone before she realized it was still in the bottom of Waylen's car along with a week's worth of groceries. "What time is it?"

Nick gestured to the dashboard. "Ten-thirty."

"I need to get home *now*."

"You have a funny way of saying thank you."

Lia glared at him. "Why should I say thank you to a guy who pushed me and didn't even stop to apologize?"

Nick grimaced. "I *am* sorry about that, but I'm also the guy who saved your life."

He had a point. "If you get me home, then I'll call it even. But don't think this gets you out of telling me what you know."

"Have you ever stopped to think maybe you were safer not knowing?"

She had, and that's what worried her.

CHAPTER FOUR

FLASHING RED AND blue police lights captured Lia's attention as Nick turned down her street. *What are they doing?* Leaning her head out the window, Lia counted the number of houses to see where they were parked. "Stop here." She frantically pulled the door handle. When it didn't budge, she shouted at Nick, "Let me out!"

"Okay, okay. Relax."

The van stopped, and Lia jumped out. Slashing pain radiated up and down her legs. She gasped but rushed on, trying to ignore each excruciating step. The police were parked in front of her house. *Not again. Please, please, not again.* The door was open. Music from a cartoon spilled outside. Lia sprinted to the porch, slowing as she neared the front door. *What if she's hurt? What if she's dead?* Her mind conjured macabre images from her mom's accident. "Lucy?"

She was sitting with her legs crossed in front of the tv. The remote control and plate of cookies sat next to her. She looked up and smiled. "You're back!"

Lia's shoulder sagged with relief. She gave her sister a tight squeeze, looked around the house and frowned. Nothing seemed out of place. A toilet flushed, and instead of Waylen, E.J. walked out the bathroom.

"What are you doing here?"

"I stopped by to see you and found her here all by herself. What the hell, Lia?"

"What do you mean *by herself*? Where's Waylen?"

"I don't know."

Lia put her head in her hands and sank onto the couch. Relief and anger both warred inside her, each fighting to take control. Relief won out. "He probably left to go to work."

"That doesn't make it right. She's only five years old! Anything could've happened to her."

"I know, I know."

"Where were you?"

"I went to the store to get some groceries."

E.J. was looking at her with narrowed eyes. "Then where are they?"

Lia took a minute to think. The truth would either make her sound delusional or paranoid, and she didn't really understand what had happened in the first place. She stuck with the facts. "In the back of Waylen's car. On Haven road.... It broke down."

Lia got up, dragging her feet as she walked. Her arm ached, and she needed some quiet to think. Lia dropped her purse on the floor and reached into her dresser for a tube of arnica cream. Lia rubbed the cool lotion into her skin, but stopped when E.J. walked into the room and shut the door. "Where else did you go?"

"Nowhere."

"You have blood on your shoes. You don't go nowhere and end up with blood on your shoes."

Lia stilled and looked down. Dark, rusty blood was staining the tips of her converse, bleeding faintly into the bright--green material. Flecks were splattered across the laces. She looked up at E.J. and knew he could see the lie forming on her face. They had been friends too long; he knew her too well.

"Where did you go, Ophelia? What happened?"

The simple act of saying her full name told Lia how serious he was. Any attempt at a lie would be unforgivable. But how could she possibly tell him the truth when she didn't even know what it was?

"I saw something," she breathed. "Something I shouldn't. Something that can't be real."

"Tell me."

"You'll think I'm crazy." She felt for the bed and collapse on it, her legs shaking.

"I already think you're crazy."

"I went to the Clover to talk to the landlord about some late rent payments, and on the way home, Anita stopped me. She got sick, really sick, and as I was calling for help, someone tried to drag me out of the car." The more she talked about it, the more she shook, like her body was trying to rid itself of the memory. "I fought and screamed for help, but no one came. At least not right away. They knocked me to the ground and... Anita...."

She hadn't even called anyone about Anita yet. What if she was still there? What if she was suffering alone? *I'm a horrible person. I'm shit. I only thought about myself.* She paced back and forth. "I need to call someone. The sheriff's office."

"Lia, hold on."

"Wait, there were cars out front when I got home." She was halfway down the hall when E.J. put a hand on her shoulder and brought her to stop. He turned her to face him. "Why are there police cars outside?"

"I think you're in shock. You need to sit down."

"I can't! I can't leave her there when she needs me! Everybody needs me." Her voice cracked and E.J.'s eyes softened.

"Lia." E.J. pulled her into a tight hug while the last bit of self-control she had slipped away. She could feel the emotions clawing their way to the surface, like an animal that had been held in captivity finally finding the door to its cage left unlocked. Wild, enormous and something she couldn't begin to handle. She was a ball of yarn, slowly starting to unravel.

"Don't," she whispered. She balled her hands into the material of his shirt and buried her face in his shoulder. "Please, I can't." Her words came out hoarse and strangled.

"It's going to be okay."

Lia shut her eyes as the sobs came and the shame followed.

Always ashamed. Always sorry. Always weak. Her mom's words echoed in her head. *There isn't one person you can count on in this world. No one's going to stick their neck out to help you, and trusting people only earns you a knife in the back. Remember, baby girl. The only person you should ever rely on is you. You're the only person who won't let you down.*

E.J. had never hurt her and had always been there for her. She hated how, even as he literally held her upright, she didn't completely trust him. Deep down, Lia was terrified she'd never be able to trust anyone. She was haunted by her mom's bitterness and anger. She was held captive by fear of Waylen and his cruelty. *Will I ever be normal?* How would she function in the world when she was constantly questioning the motives of everyone around her?

Lia wiped her eyes and saw Lucy watching from her spot in front of the TV, wringing her hands and chewing her bottom lip. Lia stepped away from E.J. and opened her arms. Lucy flung herself into them, holding onto Lia for dear life, holding on to her like at any moment she might disappear. The affection stilled the storm inside her, calmed her, and pulled her back together. It gave Lia hope there might be something inside of her worthwhile, whole and lovable after all.

"I need your help, E.J."

LIA TOLD E.J. everything in whispers as they sat at the kitchen table. She wasn't sure what he believed, but in true E.J. style, he went after the problem he knew he could handle first. "Have you talked to anyone from Waylen's work, like Lance said to do? He could be bullshitting."

Lia stiffened. Hurt coursed through her, and when she spoke, she chose her words carefully. They still came out shaking with anger. "Are you defending Waylen?"

"No, of course not."

Lia never had much of a poker face, and the disbelief must have shown. E.J. reached out for her hand, but she sat back in her chair and crossed her arms. *I don't need to be coddled.* She didn't need to be pitied or comforted, she needed to be believed. He frowned. "I just think that if we're going to go to the sheriff's department about this, we need to have all the proof we can get."

"The sheriff's department? Are you crazy?!" She was halfway out of her chair before she realized she'd shouted. Lucy looked up from playing with a set of plastic blocks that E.J. had brought over. Lia sank back down and lowered her voice. "They are *never* going to believe me."

"You don't know that——"

Lia raised a hand to stop him. "Actually, I do. Don't you think my mom tried to tell them what was going on? Waylen's family owns half of the properties downtown, and his brother works in the department. Not only did they not believe us, they told him about it so that when we got home...." She shut her eyes against the memory and swallowed hard.

E.J. slammed his fist on the table, making her jump. "Sorry," he said without looking up. "I just hate that this was going on for years without anybody doing something. I was your friend for fifteen years, and I never suspected anything."

Lia got up and went around the table so that she was facing him. "Hey, don't blame yourself for this. You were just a kid. There wasn't anything you could've done."

She had never talked to anyone about this, and she couldn't help feel regret that she told E.J.. It mixed with the waves of helplessness, everything churning together like a sour whirlpool in her stomach. *He isn't going to be able to help me, and now he's going to have to live with that. He's going to have to carry the burden of my secret. I'm a horrible person.* Her chest ached as more emotions tried to claw their way free. She fought for air as her throat tightened. *Am I not going to be happy until everyone around me suffers? Is this what Waylen feels? Am I like him?*

The idea made her feel sick and violated. She had grown up with him for most of her life. It would make sense that there was something of him in her, like learned behavior. Or maybe it went deeper than that. The thought that she might not be able to trust herself was terrifying. She pushed back the fear and gave her attention to E.J. "Whatever. It's too far in the past for anyone to do anything about anyway. It's like a story that happened to someone else, like an alternate-universe Lia. Like another person in another room."

This time E.J. really did look at her like she was crazy. "What, you don't care?"

Lia huffed in frustration. "I'm saying I can get past it. Sure, it messed me up, but I know I'll find a place where I'm okay. Not forgiveness, I'm not that strong of a person. Acceptance. I accept that it happened." She looked toward the living room again, where Lucy was playing. She curled her fists. "What I can't accept is sitting back while the same thing happens to Lucy….I'd rather die." It might have seemed dramatic, but Lia knew in her heart it was the truth.

E.J. was quiet for a minute, and when he did speak Lia almost couldn't hear him. "I'm scared that if you stay here, you will."

He began to cry. He did it without making a sound, the way Lia had taught herself to do, and if it wasn't for the fact that she was sitting in front of him, she wouldn't have been able to tell. She had only ever seen him cry once before, and the sight of it had made her cry with him. She felt that same urge now and wrapped her arms around him, protecting him from onlookers, even though no one besides Lucy was there to see. She wanted to return the privacy and comfort he had given her only a half hour earlier. His forehead pressed against her cheek. It was hot and clammy.

"Are you feeling okay? Health-wise, I mean."

E.J. scrubbed his face with the bottom of his shirt, and Lia had the decency to pretend nothing had happened. He shrugged. "I'm getting a cold. Nothing a little cold syrup can't fix."

"And rest."

"Which I will get tomorrow."

"Why not tonight?"

E.J. produced a familiar megawatt smile that in every instance in the history of their friendship had come right before a whole world of trouble. "I have a date tonight."

Lia resisted rolling her eyes, but just barely. "Seriously, a date? A date is worth risking your health over?"

"With Nicole Cates? Absolutely."

Lia perked up a bit at that. She liked Nicole. Out of all the neighborhood girls they'd grown up with, she had been the least mean to Lia and was generally a good person, as far as she could tell. "I approve."

"Not like I was asking for it, but thanks."

"Trust me, if I needed to, I could make life hell for the people you dated."

E.J. scoffed, and Lia raised her eyebrows. "You're telling me that if someone you were dating talked smack about me you wouldn't have a problem with it?"

"Absolutely. As soon as I was done sleeping with her, I'd drop her like yesterday's news."

Lia picked up the nearest dish towel and flung it at him.

"You're disgusting!"

He ducked, laughing. "No, I'm honest. I would hope that you could be the bigger person long enough that it doesn't interfere with my sex life. I would do the same for you."

"You better not treat Nicole like that. You shouldn't treat anyone like that," she said after thinking about it. "Promise me you'll get some rest as soon as you can. There's enough people ending up in the hospital as it is."

At the mention of the sicknesses, E.J.'s face fell. "About that. Remember how you asked me why the cops are parked across the street?"

Lia nodded. She had forgotten all about that in the emotional chaos of the day.

"It's Mrs. Ryan. She's missing."

FOR THE SECOND time that day, Lia considered all the bad things that could've happened if E.J. hadn't decided to drop by. *What if the police had found Lucy home alone by herself instead*

of him? Being the last person to have talked to Mrs. Ryan, it wasn't a gigantic leap to assume the police would want to question her. "Do they have any idea what happened?"

E.J. shook his head. "The rumor going around is that the sheriff can't get a hold of anyone in Willowpoint. The phones just ring."

There was something troubling Lia. It had happened before, like a word stuck on the tip of her tongue. She stuck her head in her hands."Willowpoint...." She sat up. "The bleeding bride!"

"O-kay, I'm gonna need to buy a vowel."

Lia told him about her unsettling encounter with the woman at the hospital. It was difficult to convey how scary it had been up close, but E.J. looked spooked all the same. "Then Mrs. Ryan mentioned she had a client meeting in Willowpoint. I didn't even put it together until now."

"Something's not right. All this stuff with Willowpoint, and then you almost get killed by two guys who just happened to find you on that road with Anita. I want to help Mrs. Ryan, but I think it would be better if the three of us get out of here for awhile."

"What?"

"You said it yourself; nobody's going to believe that

Waylen's bad news until he slips up, probably in front of witnesses. I'd rather not have you and Lucy on the receiving end of that. Maybe if we go somewhere else, some place with different resources, they can tell us what to do. And if these mystery men are really trying to shut you up, then it will be a whole lot harder if we're on the move."

"There's one problem, though. If Waylen catches wind of this he's going to lose it. He'll do anything to keep Lucy."

"It's a definite risk," E.J. agreed. "But can you really afford to stay here?"

Lia thought back to what Nick had told her. *Everyone's life is in danger.* She didn't know exactly what he meant by that, but along with everything else, it didn't bode well. "No, I don't think I can."

"Just start getting things together. After my date with Nicole, I'll swing by and you can pretend I'm helping organize the church rummage sale or something. We can move your stuff without him being none the wiser. Win-win for everyone."

She doubted it would be that simple. Still, the look of fierce determination on E.J.'s face told her he would see this through, no matter what. The strength of his conviction quelled most of her fears. "I'll start right after you leave."

Lia was careful about what she packed and when. She grabbed things from the back of their closets, stuff that hadn't been worn in awhile or wouldn't be missed. Packing Lucy's things was definitely trickier, because she liked to play dress up and changed her clothes many times throughout the day. The last thing she needed was for her to complain about a missing yellow sun dress or green polka dotted hoodie in front of her dad.

She was rummaging through Lucy's toy box for some idea of what she could smuggle out that would keep her sister occupied when Waylen's voice drifted through the house. He was back early. Her heart skipped a beat. Lia looked at the mess of clothes around her. She couldn't possibly clean it all up in time. Frantically shoving a few items of clothing into a secondhand barely used backpack, she chucked it under the bed as his footsteps reached the doorway. She tried not to look guilty as he towered over her, his eyes wide in surprise. Something chaotic moved behind them. Like an oncoming storm. Lia wanted to curl into a ball and disappear.

"What the hell are you doing?"

She flinched. "Just checking to make sure these still fit. The church's clothing drive is starting soon, and I wanted to go through our clothes and see if there was anything to donate."

"Those clothes were bought with *my* money, for *my* daughter. You want to help out so bad, you can start by going through your own clothes."

"I am. I'm doing mine next." *Can he tell I'm lying?* Her palms sweat, and she resisted rubbing them down the front of her jeans. *Don't look at the bed. Don't give anything away. Just stay calm.* She watched as his shoulders relaxed and whatever had come over him bled away. The shaking replaced it, and Lia's heart pitched with concern. He looked lost, like a little boy.

"Just clean this up," he said before walking to his room. The door slammed shut, echoing down the hallway.

A whirlpool of emotions raged inside Lia. *How can I feel sorry for him when he's done nothing but hurt me? He ruined my life, or at least the start of it anyway. Why do I care?* She wanted to say it was because of Lucy. She would never be able to look at her sister without seeing him, and she could never completely hate someone who was part of bringing her into the world. Lia wished that was all it was. The truth was, even though he destroyed her childhood, he also made her love him as the only father she'd had. Love. Hate. Confusion. *Why? Why was he so cruel? Why were there moments where he was kind?* She never understood this shade of gray. It wasn't fair. He didn't get to take from people like that and get to have everything he wanted.

Anger and indignation boiled under her skin, and blood pounded in her ears. *He didn't even mention Lucy.* Lia stomped down the hall and pounded on the bedroom door. Waylen wrenched it open, his eyes flashing dangerously. "What?"

"Do you even care that Lucy was left by herself today?"

"I told you I had to go to work. It isn't my fault that I can't count on you to be responsible for once."

Lia laughed humorlessly. "For once? I'm responsible for her all the time! I'm the one who watches her all day. I'm the one who takes care of her. I was one who raised her when YOU ABANDONED HER!"

Lia hadn't felt the punch. One minute she was facing Waylen and the next she was on the floor as her vision swam and her hearing went fuzzy.

"You ungrateful little bitch. You don't have anything that's your own. You live in this house because I let you. You have your job because people feel sorry for you. The only reason you get to spend time with Lucy is because *I allow it.* You would be on the street if it wasn't for me."

As Lia struggled to stand, Waylen crouched low and patted her bruised cheek. "Why do you keep pushing me, Lia? You wouldn't be in pain right now if you would just act right. That's all I'm trying to teach you. Your mom could never learn that. She thought it was okay to separate a child from her father….She was wrong." Waylen helped Lia to stand and then to the bathroom. Once she was seated on the edge of the tub, he let go. Lia was still too shocked to speak and didn't pull away as he enveloped her in a hug. "I'm sorry I lost my temper, okay? Just do what I tell you from now on. Clean yourself up."

He left, shutting the door behind him. Lia tested her legs before she stood. The room was back in focus but it looked too bright. Like a dream. Or a nightmare. Her face throbbed and nausea roiled within her. She clutched the sink for support and stared at her reflection. Her face looked unfamiliar, red and swollen, her gaze unfocused. It was difficult to tell who she saw. Was it herself? Or was it her mom?

Lia was scared Waylen was starting to forget the difference …and so was she.

CHAPTER FIVE

AFTER WAYLEN WENT to bed, Lia curled up on the couch and waited for E.J. Her duffel bag and Lucy's backpack were packed and lying at her feet. She had decided that once E.J. showed up, she was taking Lucy and never coming back. No matter what Waylen decided to try. The only thing that mattered now was not getting caught. She tapped her foot against the floor in a frantic rhythm. *It's almost two in the morning. Where is he?*

Headlights flashed through the window, and then loud knocking sounded on the front door. Lia started. She leaped towards it, pulling it open without bothering to check who it was. "What are you doing? I thought you said we were going to—?"

Instead of E.J., Nicole Cates stood there. Mascara streaked down her cheeks and her eyes were red and puffy. "Lia, I'm so sorry!" She collapsed into incoherent sobs as Lia's brow tightened in confusion.

"That's okay."

Nicole shook her head vehemently. "No, it's E.J. He's in the hospital."

"What? No, he's not. I just saw him earlier."

Nicole continued as if Lia hadn't spoken. "We were in the middle of our date, and he just…. collapsed. His dad's with him now. E.J. said he was going to stop by here after, and I didn't want you waiting for him and not know."

Lia's world pin-holed. *This can't be happening.* She turned and ran, picking up her phone and dialing E.J.'s number. With each ring, the feeling of dread in her stomach grew. *Hi, you've reached E.J. I'm not able to answer your call. You know what to do.* The beep sounded and Lia found it hard to speak. Her throat swelled. Her voice came out hoarse. "E.J. I—Nicole's here, and she's saying you're hurt or in the hospital. I don't know if this is some sick joke, but please, call me back. You have to call me back. I can't—this was all your idea. I can't do this without you.

I can't lose—"

I can't lose anyone else. Lia was on the floor again. She looked down and saw she was still clutching her phone. She didn't even know if the phone call had ended or if it was still recording. Time seemed disjointed, skipping randomly and moving ahead without her. *Is this what insanity feels like?* She jumped as a hand touched her shoulder. It was Nicole. "Maybe you should lie down?"

"Yeah." Sleep sounded like the most wonderful idea in the world. Too many shocks to the system left Lia sluggish and lethargic. Instead of walking to her room, Lia collapsed onto the couch. Her body felt heavy, and even talking felt like work. Everything was too much. Something touched her feet. She kicked, but it was just Nicole untying her shoes. "You don't need to do that."

"It's okay." She sniffed. *Was she crying again?* "It's the least I can do. I have to do something."

She knew how it felt to need to take care of someone else so you didn't focus on your own grief. "Whatever happened to E.J. wasn't your fault. He's going to be okay." *He has to be okay.*

She nodded and set Lia's shoes on the floor. "I should get

going. I don't want my mom to worry." Lia envied her. "Do you need anything before I go?"

Lia almost said no, but then she remembered the bags sitting on the floor. "This is going to sound weird, but can you keep these in your car for a day or two?" She propped herself up on her elbow and pointed to them.

"Um, yeah. Sure." Nicole slung the backpack over her shoulder just as light flooded the room. Lia peeked over the back. Waylen was standing there. Her stomach clenched.

"Will someone explain to me what's going on here?"

"Hi, Mr. Lancaster." Nicole gave him a half smile. "I was just making sure Lia was okay."

"Why wouldn't she be?"

"E.J.'s in the hospital," Lia said angrily. She sat up and almost kicked her duffel bag in the process. *Maybe if I'm careful, he won't see it.*

"Oh. Well, get off the couch. You're not sleeping in here. You're an adult."

Lia didn't understand what one thing had to do with the other, but she stood up anyway. "Let me walk you out, Nicole."

"That's okay, I got it." She picked up Lia's duffel bag and

walked to the door.

"Nicole." Waylen's voice made them both freeze. "Going somewhere?" He gestured to the bags.

She smiled that half smile again. "My parents are thinking about taking a camping trip. Anyway, see you Lia."

Lia shut and locked the front door after Nicole left. She was trapped. She felt Waylen's stare burning a hole into the back of her neck. She turned and glared at him. "Goodnight."

She pushed past him so she could get to her room. Waylen opened his mouth but Lia cut him off before he could say anything. "My best friend is in the hospital, and I have no idea why. It's two in the morning, I'm exhausted and I just want to get some sleep. So unless you feel the need to punch me again, I have nothing to say to you." Anger erased the fear.

Lia found Lucy sleeping diagonally across her mattress. Shaking her head, Lia slid her over and climbed in. She heard the sound of Waylen moving around the house. First, it was a jingle of keys. Then the sound of the door opening and finally, the sound of an engine. *Where could he be going?* An invisible weight lifted from her shoulders.

The night settled in around her, and she drifted asleep to the sound of crickets. Memories of the day flooded in and unwound like a film in reverse, the sound bites clipped and jarring. Soon, she couldn't tell if she was awake or dreaming. Somewhere in between, she dreamed of jungle cats.

It was the noise that woke her—a low, guttural growl, soft at first and then louder as Lia slowly woke up. She shook her head, trying to dismiss the last echoes of her dream, but then she froze. Two yellow eyes stared at her from the dark doorway. This was real. *What?* As moonlight spilled into her room she glimpsed its spotted coat. Instinctively, she pulled Lucy to her. They stayed that way for a while, the jaguar locking eyes with Lia as she held her breath. She knew she should do something. She should yell, reach across to the nightstand and call for help on her cell phone; but any movement could cause it to attack. Her heart pounded. *What was it that they always say in nature documentaries? Do I stare at it or not?* She felt compelled to reach out and touch the animal. She needed to convince herself it was actually real, but if it was, that would be incredibly dangerous. *Not to mention stupid.*

After awhile, Lia swallowed, gathered her courage and slowly slipped out of bed, grabbing Lucy and carrying her toward the door. Her muscles clenched in fear. As she stood before the jaguar, she waited for it to attack. But it just bowed its head and stepped aside. She took a risk and ran past it. Strangely, the animal didn't move, but its eyes followed her all the way out of the house. The only place she could think to go was E.J.'s. She set Lucy down on E.J.'s porch and pounded on the door until lights came on inside. Eddie opened the door, a concerned look on his face. *He's probably just gotten back from the hospital.*

"This is going to sound crazy, but there's a jaguar loose in my house, and I need to come in."

His eyes widened. *Great, he probably thinks I'm a basket case.* In all fairness, Lia wasn't so sure she wasn't having a mental breakdown. He stepped aside and pushed open the door. "Get inside, now."

"Thank you. I'm so sorry if—"

"Now, Lia!"

Startled, she picked up Lucy and rushed inside. Eddie slammed the door behind them and locked it. "Eddie, what's wrong?"

"Put Lucy on the couch and come here," he whispered. Lia did and joined him in front of the living room window. He pressed a finger to his lips, indicating they needed to be quiet.

Lia peered out the window and placed a hand over her mouth. She almost screamed. A pack of wolves were slowly stalked down the road, and just in front of Eddie's house, a bear was digging through his trash. They moved away from the window, and Lia whispered, "What do you think is going on?"

"I don't know."

"Black Ridge Falls doesn't even have a zoo. Where did they come from?"

Eddie smiled, but it wasn't enough to hide his exhaustion. "Is E.J. okay? Nicole came by and told me what happened."

He sank into an armchair and gestured for Lia to take the other. "I don't know."

"What do you mean?"

"They wouldn't let me see him, and no one would tell me anything. I was going to go up there again in the morning."

"I could understand them not telling *me* anything, but you're family. You're his dad."

Eddie sighed. "There's been strange things going on here for weeks. Do you remember when the two girls collapsed? I went up there to see if they were okay. I was their employer, and I was concerned. I wanted to see if there was anything I could do.

Their parents were treated the same way."

"What happens if they still won't talk to you?"

"Then I go to see the sheriff. Someone has to know something about what's going on."

It occurred to Lia that she might know who that was and one way or another, she was going to get some answers.

CHAPTER SIX

SOMETIMES LIVING IN a town as small as theirs had its perks. After Lia bribed Nancy Cates with a hand-delivered lunch from Overboard, it wasn't difficult to ask her what room the new arrivals were staying in. The Seabreeze wasn't very big or fancy, but Nancy and Jared worked hard to run a motel that was inviting, comfortable and clean. As Lia passed each sherbet-- orange painted door, the more nervous she grew. Once she had reached the last room in the line, she knocked before she could talk herself out of being there or creating any more "worst-case scenarios" in her head. The door opened a sliver showing a glimpse of the platinum and bubblegum--pink of mystery girl's hair. "We're too broke to buy anything, we know who we're voting for and we've found Jesus," she said. "So unless you're handing out free booze, go away."

"I was hoping you'd take free lunch instead."

"Oh, it's you." She unlocked the door, opening it the rest of the way and stepped aside to let Lia in.

The room was pale yellow with blue furniture. Mystery girl kicked bags and boxes out of the way as she moved across the room and banged twice on the door to what Lia assumed was the bathroom. "I'm Shiner," she said, extending her hand.

Lia shook it. "Lia."

"I know."

"You know?"

"Yep." A small table in the corner overflowed with maps and stacks of papers. Shiner began clearing some of it out of the way until she realized there was nowhere else to put it. She quickly gathered it all and carried it pile by pile into the bedroom. "Sorry about the mess, but it's been awhile since we were able to spread out. It doesn't help that neither of us were neat to begin with, or I'm assuming Nick wasn't. I really don't know."

That was interesting. "How long have you known each

other?" Lia pulled the containers out of the bag and set them on the table. Since she didn't know what they liked or how, she left it up to them to make their own plates.

"About a year," Shiner answered, returning to the room. "But I think Nick wants to be the one to explain all this to you. He likes thinking he's in charge. Helps with his fragile ego."

"Oh." *What have I gotten myself into?*

Shiner grabbed a stack of paper plates off the coffee maker and served herself. She glanced back at Lia. "Aren't you going to have any?"

"I'm not hungry." It was true. Since hearing the news about E.J., Lia hadn't felt much of anything except tired.

Nick walked into the living room and did a double take. "What are you doing here?"

"Who cares? She brought lunch! Free lunch." Shiner waved a fork at the food.

Nick buried his head in his hands. When he looked up again, it was to glare at Lia "How did you even know where we were staying?"

"Little tip? When you leave an anonymous note on someone's door, make sure you don't use the motel stationary."

"Well, I guess since you're here, it means something happened."

"If you define *something* as missing people, sick people that no one will talk about and oh yeah, packs of wild animals wandering the streets, then yeah, something's happened. And I'm not leaving here until you tell me what you know."

"Lia."

"Don't tell me I'd be safer not knowing. If you wanted to keep me safe, you'd be about twenty years too late."

Nick strode over to Lia and grasped her under the arms. Indignation flashed through her. "Hey!"

When she recovered from her shock long enough to stand, he picked up her purse and held it out to her. "Do yourself a favor and go home. You don't need to get involved in this."

"No."

"Do you want me to throw you out of here? Because I will."

Lia straightened up and clenched her fists. He couldn't boss her around, and she wasn't afraid of him. *Arrogant jerk.* "Try me."

Shiner was sitting sideways in her seat, watching them with a smirk on her face. "I hate to interrupt this teen drama moment with some reality, but seriously, Nick, we aren't making much progress on our own. It would help to have some insider knowledge."

Nick gestured to Lia. "Do you want to get her killed?"

"Without us, this whole town is as good as dead anyway."

Lia threw her hands in air. "Will somebody please tell me what's going on?"

"Someone is conducting experiments to turn people into animals and they're doing it using the water supply."

Yeah, right. Lia was startled into laughter. Not an amused laugh, either. She laughed so hard that tears streamed down her cheeks and her sides ached. It was nice to cry for a good reason for a change. She wiped her eyes. "Okay. You've had your fun. Now tell me what's really going on."

Nick's grim expression remained unchanged. Even Shiner was staring at her intently. "It's the truth."

Lia stared back at them, her eyes going wide. *Oh God, they're crazy. They're crazy and no one knows where I am.* "Look, I came here thinking you might know something that could help my friend. Obviously, I shouldn't have bothered you. Enjoy the food."

Heading for the door, she was almost there before Nick spun her around so that her back was pressed against the door. "How long ago did your friend get sick?"

"Last night."

"Let me guess; they aren't telling the family anything."

Lia shook her head. "His dad was going to go back there today."

"Then let me tell you what's going to happen. He has about two weeks left before he's dead. It'll be slow, painful and in the end, the thing they bury isn't even going to look like the person you knew. Are you willing to risk saving his life just because you don't want to believe us?"

Lia chewed her bottom lip. "Do you have any proof?"

"We can show you," said Shiner. "But we need to get into the hospital."

Taking a ride to the hospital didn't sound all that complicated, but she had a feeling they would be going to an area that wasn't exactly open to the public.

As they drove to the hospital, Lia stared out the window and absentmindedly tapped her foot. As the three of them strode through the lobby to the main elevators she was struck by a burst of anxiety. Her eyes darted to the security cameras, and she picked at her cuticles. Nick reached over and took her hand. "Just act natural."

He placed a strand of hair behind her ear and Lia jerked

away from him. "Don't touch me."

Nick frowned, and her stomach dropped. She could help but pull away when people touched her. Waylen actions taught her to fear everything, even gentle touches. *He shouldn't touch me anyway. He's way too relaxed about getting into people's personal space.* Was that normal?

They walked into the empty elevator and when she looked to see what floor they were going to. Shiner pressed level 3—the same floor as her mom. The elevator rose, and Lia's stomach flip flopped uncomfortably. She looked at Nick to find him staring at her. She made a face at him. "What?"

"That bruise looks new."

Lia raised a hand to it without thinking. "It is." Her cheeks flushed. She found it hard to look at him after that and focused on a far corner of the purplish-gray carpet. The small vibrations as the elevator climbed made Lia want to cling to the railing. The elevator stopped with a sudden jolt, and she nearly fell into Nick. He unclasped his hand from hers and held her steady.

Standing in front of them, Shiner snickered. "You two are so awkward."

The doors opened. A nurse Lia had never seen before sat at

the front desk, and she blew out a relieved breath. *So far, so good.*
Lia avoided eye contact with her as they hurried past. Instead of
turning right, where Lia's mom was, they turned left. *Oh no.*
Around the corner was a gray security door, and they didn't have
an access card. *What are we going to do now? It's not like we can
steal one.* Nick casually glanced over his shoulder at the nurse
and then again down the other end of the hall. "You're clear."

Shiner stepped to the key pad and pulled a card from the
pocket of her overalls. She swiped it. The door buzzed loudly,
swinging open. Nick pushed her in the back when she didn't
move. The lady at the front desk had risen from her chair and
was approaching. Lia picked up the pace.

"In here," Shiner called from somewhere ahead of them.

Nick and Lia sprinted down another hall and found Shiner
standing in the doorway of an open exam room. Ten beds lined
one wall with another ten facing opposite. Each one had a gauzy
blue curtain drawn around it, but Lia could still hear the chug
and beeping of different machines. "You keep watch," Shiner
said to Nick. He nodded and disappeared outside the doorway.
Another wave of apprehension skittered up her spine when Nick
was out of sight. It was easier when he goaded her into putting

up a brave front. Now she just felt exposed. She crossed her arms against the chill of the air-conditioning.

Shiner looked over at Lia. "Are you ready?"

No. "Ready?"

"We're here to see your friend. What's his name?"

"Eduardo Rodriguez Jr.—E.J."

"I'm going to go look for him. You can wait here if you want."

Lia shook her head. "I'll look with you."

"Pick a door."

"A door?"

"Like on those old game shows? I guess it would be better to say *pick a curtain.*"

She's making fun of this? My best friend's in here somewhere. Lia scowled at her.

"C'mon Lia, lighten up. You'll never get through this if you don't."

"Why is it that you and Nick feel the need to tell me what to do?"

Shiner rolled her eyes. "Whatever. I'm not looking for a fight."

She moved toward the first bed and stepped behind the curtain. Lia, not feeling friendly towards her, chose a bed on the opposite side. Lia's stomach was in knots. *It can't be as horrible as they're saying. It'll be fine.* Her hands shook from nerves. She pulled back the curtain and screamed. The man in the bed was like nothing she had ever seen before. Boils covered the inflamed skin around his eye sockets. The milky white of his left eye was complete showing, as if it had rolled back into his head. Bone stuck out of right arm, twisted backwards at a ninety--degree angle. His left leg bent backward. Black patches of hair sprouted all over his face and body, while only a few strands of hair remained on his scalp. When he saw her, he opened his other eye. It had gone completely black. His lips were cracked, and when he tried to speak, drool and blood ran over them down his chin. He raised his undamaged hand to point at her, and she was struck by how skeletal it was. *Oh my God! Are they claws? Talons?*

Lia shrieked again as a hand slapped over her mouth. "Are you trying to get us caught?" Shiner hissed in her ear.

Lia shook her head and Shiner removed her hand. "He—" She struggled to control her voice. "He doesn't even look *human.*"

"I know. It scared me too when I first saw it. Some of them don't survive the mutation and some of them get stuck in between." They looked at the man. He still had his finger outstretched, emitting rattling groans as if he was trying to tell them something. "I think death is much kinder than this."

"Do you think E.J.— ?" The thought was too terrible to finish.

Shiner shook her head. "He doesn't look too bad, but it's still early for him."

"You found him?"

Shiner nodded. "He's over here."

Lia paused at the edge of the curtain. *What if this is all I'll see when I remember him? I don't want to remember him like this. I don't want my last memory of him to be filled with fear.* Lia shook herself. *I'm going to save him. I'm not going to let him end up like that.*

Lia steeled herself and slowly pulled back the edge of the curtain. *Does this mean they're telling the truth? And if it is, what's going to happen to the rest of us?*

All thought fled from her mind as Lia stared down at E.J. *He looks like a skeleton.* Gray tinged his brown skin. His gaunt face and emaciated body hardly made an impression in the mattress and pillow, and his skin stretched over his bones like plastic wrap. Lia brushed his charcoal hair out of his eyes. Warmth radiated under her palm. He was burning up. "It's barely been twenty-four hours." Despair clawed at the back of her throat, but she was pleased at how steady her voice sounded. "Why is he this bad?"

"Everyone's body reacts differently to the virus. Maybe his is just fighting it more."

As Lia moved her hand, her fingertips brushed against something rough near his shoulder. She leaned forward to get a closer look. A row of horizontal lines marked E.J.'s neck. She ran a finger across them. They felt jagged, like cuts or scratches, except without inflammation or bleeding. *I don't remember seeing these yesterday.* "Shiner, look at this."

Shiner peered at the marks. Her eyes widened, sliding down to E.J.'s chest and back again. "They're moving in sync with his breathing." Her voice was hushed, almost as if in awe.

Lia saw it, too. The cuts were expanding as he breathed, each flap of skin lifting as his chest filled with air.

"I wonder if…." Shiner pressed a hand to the cuts. E.J.'s breaths grew ragged and he gasped. Shiner moved her hand, and his breathing returned to normal.

What just happened? "What does that mean?"

"I'm not sure. This is just a hunch, but I think his body is accepting the mutation. Not fighting it."

"You mean he's….?"

"Turning into something. Those marks? I'd swear they're gills."

"Like a fish?"

"No, like an antelope."

Lia shot her a withering glance. *Like she knows everything.* "Well, what does that mean? Is he going to be okay?"

"Oh, sure. Just buy him a gallon tank and some coral, and he'll be good as new."

Lia clenched her jaw as fury overwhelmed her. "Shut up! Obviously you don't know what it's like to care about people, but my best friend is fighting for his life. Something I can't even begin to wrap my mind around. So unless you can contribute something other than sarcasm, just shut the hell up!"

"Hey." Nick stuck his head in the doorway. "A little louder. I don't think the people on the eighth floor heard you yet."

"Nick, come take a look at this," said Shiner, ignoring Lia completely. Lia seethed.

Nick walked over while Shiner took his place as lookout. He whistled. "I didn't think it was possible. A mammal to fish mutation. They are going to lose it."

"They?" Like Shiner, Nick didn't answer her. She tried again. "Is he going to...survive?"

Nick ran a hand through his hair. "It depends. The one

thing I know for sure is that we need to get him out of here. The people who did this are going to want to study him, and we can't let them. His only chance of surviving is if he comes with us."

"Why? Who are they? And go where?"

"Look, you have your proof. We can talk about everything else back at the room. We've stayed here too long already."

Lia looked at E.J. She didn't know where he was or what was happening to him, but he didn't seem to be in any pain. Still, she couldn't bring herself to leave him. *What if I blink and then he's gone?*

"Hey." Nick's voice was soft and reassuring, but it only made the anger rise up in her again.

"Don't try to talk to me like you know me. Like we're friends. We're not." *I have a friend. A best friend. And even though he's here, he's not, and there's no one else who'd understand.* She had never been good at making friends. The prospect of having to make new ones, however slight, made her want to surrender to the weariness that had settled like lead in her bones. No one could ever replace E.J.

"If you want to get caught by the hospital staff, be my guest. But we're out of here." Nick's voice was flat and cold. If she knew him at all, she might have said he was angry. He wasn't even looking at her anymore. When she didn't respond, he stormed out, yelling at Shiner when she didn't follow.

Lia never took her eyes off E.J. "They're rude, sarcastic and kinda horrible, but if there's a chance they could make you better, how am I supposed to say no?" She wasn't expecting him to answer, but he had told her that it was okay to have hope so she asked him anyway. "What do you want me to do?"

For once, she didn't have a plan, or way forward, or any idea how to cope. So, she did the only thing that made sense to her. "I'm leaving now, but I promise you that I'll come back."

As she walked down the hall, Lia could feel everything catch up with her. She hadn't ate or slept in over twenty-four hours. Hunger had stopped squeezing her stomach hours ago, but the exhaustion left her feeling like she was seeing the world from under water. He vision kept blurring and everything was bathed in a halo of bright light. She wasn't even sure if her feet were still moving, but the door was getting closer, so she supposed she was. *I'll be okay as long as I can get to the truck. The adrenaline should kick in soon, and the tiredness will disappear.*

"Are you okay?"

Lia blinked slowly and tried to focus on who was speaking.

It was taking too much effort to keep her eyes open. "Sure, I am."

Shiner gripped her arm and guided her through the gray door. *Wasn't she supposed to go with Nick? When did that door open?* Lia's thoughts were slowing down and circling each other like alphabet soup. She meant to turn and look at Shiner, but her head just kind of lolled sideways onto her shoulder instead. "You stayed."

"Nick forgets that not everyone wants his help all the time. He'll get over it."

"What?"

She sighed. "He's one of those guys that's always holding the door for people. He gets angry when people don't say thank you, even when no one asked him to hold the door in the first place. And he likes a project."

All of Lia's anger had dissolved into exhaustion, but Shiner's words still registered in her brain. "Like me?"

"Like me."

A nurse stopped in front of them and Lia's heart rebounded sharply in her chest. "We were just about to call your house." Shiner's gaze zipped back and forth between them. *She's probably deciding whether or not to run. Actually running might not be a bad idea.* "Miss Thomas?" The nurse was peering at her in concern. Lia knew her. *She's one of the women who looks after my mom.* The hollow feeling inside her turned to cement.

"Yeah?"

"I think you should come with me and have a seat over here."

"Why, what's going on?"

"Let's sit down first."

"No!" She yelled so loud that every person in the lobby was staring at her. Even Shiner looked startled. "I am sick and tired of being in the dark all the time. I'm sick of asking questions. Tell me what's going on right now!"

"I'm sorry to tell you this," she said in a hushed tone. "Your mom passed away a few minutes ago."

The devastation hit her like a ton of bricks. All of the air whooshed out of Lia's lungs. She felt light-headed, and the room swam before her eyes. "Okay." The last thing she saw was the design of the hospital floor.

CHAPTER
SEVEN

WHEN PEOPLE DIE in their sleep, do they ever realize they're no longer dreaming? It was the first thought Lia had as she slowly regained consciousness. Eddie and her sister stood at the side of the stretcher while hospital staff raced back and forth through the hallways like they were training for a marathon. Eddie's smile was warm, but his eyes seemed sad. "It's going to be okay."

Tears stung Lia's eyes, and she rushed to blink them back. *No, I don't think it is. I don't think anything is ever going to be okay again.* Grief rose upward from the pit of her stomach, pushing outward, stealing her breath, suffocating her. She didn't want the tears to come. Yet, the grief swallowed her resolve like a tidal wave, and she shook like a volcano seconds away from eruption. She wailed like a wounded animal as the sobs tore from her throat. She would leave it all here. The pain, the fear, the hope, the helplessness. Eddie held her tight in his arms like he could push it all back in again. But he couldn't. It was done. She had lost control.

Afterward, the days all seemed to blur together. Her mom's funeral was done, and Lia tried to pay attention to the people who stopped in front of her to give their condolences. Her mom didn't have any family left, so it was mostly people from town who came. Lia spotted a few of Waylen's friends from work. Even Lance, her landlord. She watched Waylen out of the corner of her eye, smiling, making jokes and shaking hands with everyone who came. She clenched her jaw so hard she thought her teeth would crack. *I wish I could punch **him** in the face. I wish E.J. were here.* Even though she knew it wasn't possible, she was glad that Eddie was.

The person at the front of the line moved, and Eddie stood face-to-face with Waylen. Waylen's smile fell, his eyes closing to slits. Eddie's shoulders tensed, and his lips thinned. "Beth-Ann was a good woman and a great mom," Eddie said. "We'll all miss her."

Eddie went to pat Lucy on the head but Waylen pulled her behind him, baring his teeth in a feral smile. "Just like I'm sure we're all going to miss your son."

A gasp of shock went through the room. Lia flushed with shame. There were few times when she had seen Eddie really lose his temper, but it wasn't something she could ever forget. She searched for someone who could help, but there was no need. Eddie glared at Waylen until Waylen's eyes dropped to the carpet. He moved towards Lia and gave her a hug. "Did either of you eat today?"

Lia shook her head. "We'll probably wait until we get back to the house. I guess Cates' organized some kind of wake."

"I'm going to be checking to make sure you do. I made both of your favorites."

Lia was stunned. "You cooked?"

"Of course I did!"

"Eddie, what about E.J.?"

With everything going on, Lia was afraid that she relied too heavily on Eddie and left him no time to be there for E.J. *He should be with E.J. now, not here.* As if sensing her thoughts, Eddie sighed. "You shouldn't worry about that. At least not today."

"But Eddie—"

"I can look after more than one family member at a time. Right now, I want to mourn the loss of your mother, because she was a dear friend of mine. Besides, she'd want me to look after her girls."

"Family member?"

Eddie placed his hands on her shoulders. "You and Lucy are part of my family, and family is everything. Understand? I'll see you back at the house."

Lia nodded and another man took his place. His green eyes were bloodshot, and his breath smelled strongly of vodka. At least his clothes looked clean. He wore a blue button-down shirt and sharply creased black dress pants. His smile revealed bright white teeth. It wasn't anyone she recognized. Lia hesitantly returned his smile. "Wow, you're as pretty as your momma."

The accent surprised her, too. It was a honeyed southern drawl. "Thank you. I don't think we've met."

"Oh, we haven't. I'm one of your dad's friends from way back. You're mom only met me a couple times."

Stepdad. "Well, thank you for coming."

"Listen, do you have a minute?"

Lia looked around for Waylen and Lucy but she didn't see them anywhere. "I don't know...." *Note to self: stop running off with sketchy strangers you don't know!* He didn't look like a monster, but the worst ones rarely did. Even Waylen seemed harmless to most untrained eyes. It also occurred to her then that the men who killed Anita were probably still looking for her. She shivered.

"We can just step right back here." He gestured to one of the middle pews on the right side of the room. *There are people here, and it wouldn't be wandering off.* She nodded and waited until he walked in front of her. Once he was seated, Lia slid in beside him, keeping a good distance between them.

"How can I help you, Mr...?"

"You can just call me Cade." He fidgeted and pulled a cigarette from his shirt pocket.

"I don't think you can smoke in here."

"Right." He put it away. "I just wanted to tell you that I'm sorry."

Lia's brows knitted together in confusion. *Why couldn't he have said that when we were up there?* "I appreciate your condolences."

He rubbed the back of his neck, and Lia noticed a familiar tremor in his hand. "Not for that. I mean, I am sorry to hear about your momma, but it's more than that. I wanted to say I'm sorry for what happened to her and for not stopping it."

Hair rose on her arms. "Stopping it?"

"From stopping Waylen that night when he made me drive him to the house. I swear, I didn't know he was going to lose it like that."

"You were there that night?" *Waylen was there that night? Why?* Lia tried to think back to what her mom had said the week the two of them argued. Hadn't she said that she kicked Waylen out the month before? Memories from the night Waylen punched her slowly trickled in. "*She thought it was okay to separate a child from her father… she was wrong.*" Lia swallowed thickly. She felt like she was going to be sick. "What'd you see?"

"He was yelling at her about how she couldn't leave him. How he wasn't gonna let her take his kid away from him. He turned around and then bam! I didn't know he was going to hit her. She went straight down. Would have been okay, I think. Except he kept going. By the time I pulled him off of her…." He shuddered.

"Why tell me and not the police?"

"Waylen said he confessed. I'm the one that brought him back here so he could do it."

"But you didn't go with him to the station or anything?"

Cade's eyes widened as he realized what she was getting at. "Shit, I thought he—Anyway, I'm sorry. I'm sorry about everything."

He rose and Lia grabbed his wrist. "Please, you were there. You could tell them."

"If they haven't figured it out by now, I'm not going to rat him out. There's no use in getting involved."

"But you are involved!"

He yanked his arm out of Lia's grip and ran for the door. She ran after him. "Wait!"

By the time she made it to the entrance, Cade was already starting his car. She stood there as he drove away. *I hope he crashes.* A hand touched her shoulder, and she spun around. It was Waylen.

"What do you say we get going? There's only a few people left anyway." The nausea she had felt earlier returned in spades. *I've been living in the house with her murderer. I've been leaving my sister alone with a murderer.* Lia doubled over and puked on his shoes.

LIA, WAYLEN AND Lucy walked in the house. Dozens of people crowded the living area, their quiet chatter a comforting welcome. Tears welled in Lia's eyes—she had never expected this. The smell of fried chicken, rich tomato sauce and spicy Mexican food wafted through the air. The only funeral Lia had ever been to (and remembered) was her grandpa, and even though he had been a resident of Black Ridge Falls all his life, Lia didn't remember the house being packed with this many people. Lia picked up Lucy, who was trying to turn up the television loud enough to hear her cartoons, and held her on her hip. "You can watch TV later, lady bug."

"But why?"

"Because we're going to spend time with all the nice people who are here to say goodbye to Mommy."

"But we already did that at the other place!"

Lia smoothed out the wrinkles in her sister's dress. "This is different. This is kinda like a party to celebrate Mommy's life."

"Like a birthday party?"

"Something like that. We sit and tell stories about her, we eat food and we remember all of the good things we love about her."

"Oh. Sissy?"

"Yes?"

"Is it okay if I don't remember Mommy?"

Lia hadn't cried since that day at the hospital, but now her eyes brimmed with tears and her throat closed up. "Yeah, that's okay. Today you'll hear all kinds of stories that will help you remember her."

Lia searched the crowd and spotted Eddie putting out food in the kitchen. "Let's go get you something to eat, huh? Maybe Eddie made some mac and cheese?"

"With ketchup!" Lucy shouted, raising a tiny fist in the air.

Lia shook her head. *Will the ketchup never end?* "I am so glad I get to be there when you tell Mr. Eddie that."

Eddie did indeed make Lucy's macaroni and cheese (with ketchup added under protest), but he had also made other things that made Lia's mouth water even though she'd had no desire to eat in days. "It's called the *Mexican sandwich.* I made these smaller than they usually are, but it's tortillas layered with rice, beans and beef, covered in gravy and melted cheese." It looked like heaven and smelled even better. Eddie placed a bowl of salsa on the table. "Do you want me to cut you a piece?"

"I can't believe after all these years you don't know the answer to that."

Eddie chuckled and slid a medium size piece unto a plate. She also asked for a piece of chicken and a tiny bit of mac and cheese. After not eating for three days, Lia found herself starving. She slid her fork into the Mexican sandwich and took a bite. It was every bit as good as she thought it would be. Nicole Cates slid into the kitchen chair between her and Lucy. "Hi, guys," she said.

Lia waved. Once her food was gone, she said, "I did tell your mom thank you for doing all this, didn't I? With all the people here, it's hard to keep track."

"You did, and she knows anyway." Nicole started pulled on the long French braid hanging over her shoulder. "I keep wanting to tell you how sorry I am, but it seems lame. Like it's not enough."

"There's never a right thing to say, but I'd rather hear I'm sorry a hundred times than nothing at all. At least, if it's honest."

"It is." Nicole reached her hand across the table to squeeze Lia's fingers. "I am so sorry your mom is gone. She was really nice and a lot of fun."

"What do you remember most about her? I want Lucy to

hear everything."

Nicole nodded, and a tiny grin pulled at the corner of her mouth. "I remember those festival pageants she used to put you in every year."

Lia groaned and covered her face with her hands. "Out of everything you could've picked, that's what you remember?"

"I'm sorry! It's just, you won like every year, and I was always so jealous of you. You always had these amazing dresses."

That did make Lia smile. "My mom made them herself. We couldn't afford to buy them, and she wanted a new one for each contest. Taught herself how to sew and everything."

"Seriously? Your mom should have gone into business."

"Yeah, but I hated those stupid pageants. I always got so nervous before I'd go on." Lia leaned a little closer to Nicole. "One time, E.J. stole some tequila from his dad's cabinet and told me to drink it before I went on. I got so drunk, I almost fell off the stage."

"What!" bellowed Eddie while she and Nicole dissolved into laughter.

"My mom was so mad."

"Yeah, I wish the two of them could be here," said Nicole.

The weight of reality settled on their shoulders, and they finished their meal in somber silence.

Later, with fuller bellies and heavier hearts, Lia took Lucy back into the living room and they sat on the couch as people reminisced with them. She laughed. She cried a little. She ached for the kind, passionate, full-of-life mom that she had known before Waylen entered their lives. But without him, they wouldn't have Lucy. Lia watched as her little sister took in the memories with wonder and joy. She probably didn't understand what was happening, but the ache in Lia's heart was lightened by the sound of sister's laugh. For just a minute, she almost believed everything would be okay. *None of these people know what really happened to her.* She gazed around the room, looking for Waylen. He was standing in the hall watching everyone while he sipped on some kind of amber liquid. Her heart sank. *He's not supposed to be drinking.*

"Lia?" One of her neighbors tapped on her shoulder. "There's a girl outside who says she needs to speak to you."

Lia made her way to the porch. Shiner and Nick were standing next to their van, watching people coming in and out of the house. She hadn't seen them since the day her mom died.

The weather was still warm, but the sun was hidden behind fluffy clouds and the scent of oncoming rain hung in the air.

"We're sorry about your Mom," said Shiner.

"Thank you."

Nick shoved his hands in his pockets. "We know the timing isn't great, but we still have a lot to talk about."

Lia folded her arms and took a step back. "I'm not going anywhere today. So whatever you have to say is going to have to wait."

"It's important," Nick said.

"This is *more* important."

"Will you just—Get in the van for a minute." Lia eyed him warily as he opened the passenger door and she climbed in. Shiner got in the back. Nick turned in his seat so he was facing her. "We think some dangerous people are coming into town soon, and I want you to keep this with you." He pressed a gun into Lia's hand. Anxiety fluttered in her stomach. She fought the urge to drop it.

"Now I know you're crazy! I'm not keeping a gun under the same roof as a five year old kid."

"I told you she'd never go for it." Shiner flipped through a fashion magazine as if this sort of thing happened every day.

"That's why I want you to have it. For protection. These

people are seriously bad news, Lia. I don't want anything to happen to you or her."

Lia considered that for a moment. "I'll keep it in my purse, but I'm not using it."

"I hope you're never in a situation to change your mind."

"So, why are these people coming here, anyway?"

"As part of a containment plan," said Shiner. "Now they're getting results, they're going to want to collect them from everyone involved."

"Without risking anyone getting out," explained Nick. "We're going to have to get E.J. out of here before they implement quarantine. They'd be watching too closely after that. I want you and Lucy to come with us."

Lia had thought about asking to come with them. She didn't want to risk leaving her best friend with a bunch of strangers. But that would've meant leaving Lucy, and she wouldn't have been able to do that. But now Nick was suggesting another way. The only problem was Waylen. *If I try to leave with her, there's a good chance he'll try to kill me.* He had done it to her mom, after all.

"What happens if we don't come with you?"

A look passed between Shiner and Nick. "You'll die," said

Shiner. "They don't like leaving loose ends."

Lia shuddered. "You mean they'd kill everyone?"

Nick nodded. "We've seen evidence of it before. They only choose small towns. Tiny populaces that are easily overlooked."

"But that means, they'll kill everyone we leave behind."

"Not if we can stop them in time," said Nick.

"Stop them how?"

"By finding a cure. We know a biochemist that's already perfected antidotes which slow the effects of the mutation, but we need more pieces for a cure."

"We need your friend," Shiner explained. "His mutation is new, and from what we can tell, it might actually be successful. The first mammal-to-fish transformation. With his genetic material we might get closer to the cure, and at the very least our biochemist could help slow his symptoms. Without it, he'll either die or turn into a fish. Either way, he'd never be human again."

It was a lot to take in, and Lia wasn't sure what she wanted to do. Nick leaned towards her. "Nobody's ever survived longer than fourteen days, and you're friend's already minus four and counting. You can't take forever, Lia."

She nodded, but just because she might leave, didn't mean

it would solve all her problems. There was still something she needed to deal with.

SHE GOT DRUNK that night. The kind of drunk that someone talked themselves into when they knew they wouldn't be able to do whatever they had in mind without it. People called it liquid courage, but Lia had always believed it was more like liquid cowardice. She supposed it didn't matter what you called it. It didn't take courage to kill a man. All you needed was a reason, and he had already given her plenty.

The house looked as belligerent as she felt. Its chipped white siding cast long, eerie shadows in the moonlight, making it look cracked all over, like it was broken. Like she had been broken. Bit by bit, he'd stolen her life until there was nothing left. Not even the lies, those misguided prayers, would stop her now. Now, she knew the truth.

A roar of anguish filled her ears as she stalked across the brittle grass, tripping up the wooden front porch, past the screen door and into the front room. The room's imposing darkness converged around her, almost as if it were sentient, holding her back or warning her away. She couldn't see the gun anymore, but she could feel the weight of it in her clammy palm. After she did this there would be no going back.

As she stumbled past pieces of furniture and hit enough end tables with her shins, she felt her way down the hall. She counted each doorknob until she found the one she was looking for. She didn't even pause. She twisted it and shoved the door open with so much force that it rebounded against the wall behind it. Her stepfather's outline rose up, and a familiar trickle of fear leaked into her brain. It told her to run, but she was through with that. She raised her arm just as he clicked on the bedside lamp.

Honey-colored light spilled over the room, illuminating the dark chestnut furniture, sandy walls and thick green carpet. Waylen looked at her then at the gun in her hand and smiled. It wasn't his pretend smile (the one he used when he tried to convince her he loved them) and it wasn't his cruel, mocking smile (the one that haunted her in her dreams.) This smile, Lia thought, looked *relieved.* Like he had been expecting her, expecting this, all along, even though she had only decided to confront him a few hours ago. Somehow, the knowledge of this scared her more than anything he could've done in that moment.

"So you know then," he said. It wasn't a question.

"Know what?" She wanted to hear him say it. She wanted an admission to what she had suspected for so long, but the look he gave her was patronizing. He quirked up an eyebrow and smirked. It was the same look he used to give her when she couldn't figure out something in her homework. The look that always seemed to say: *you know this; you just aren't trying hard enough.*

"You never could understand. It doesn't matter what you know, Lia. It all comes down to what you can *prove.*" He reached over and slid open a drawer in the nightstand. Lia tightened her grip. He pulled out a pack of cigarettes, tapped the bottom and placed one in his mouth. The hand that lit it was steady. He wasn't worried at all that she would pull the trigger. Maybe he didn't think she was a threat or, maybe because he could see how drunk she was, or both, but Lia didn't think it was either.

She was still afraid. Even with a gun aimed at his head, even with all the resolve in the world, she was paralyzed by fear. The whiskey churned in her stomach. Mixed with her fury, it ignited inside her like fire. She may hold the weapon, but he held all the power. He had all the control. And he knew it.

"What can you prove, Lia?" He dragged on his cigarette, his cerulean-blue eyes never leaving hers. Challenging her. "Do you think anyone would believe you? Did they ever? What would make this time any different?"

Over the years, she'd let herself believe that everything that had happened to her was one of those not-real things. It could just be a story. Something that faded as time went on and the memories became harder to recall. Not that she ever forgot. She knew everything that had happened because she lived it. She could remember her mom lying about the cause of all her injuries. She remembered trying to tell someone, anyone, the truth and nothing changing. She remembered fingers digging painfully into her shoulders, trying to keep her silent or else making her collaborate whatever she was told. She'd simply built a wall around it in her mind so the pain couldn't touch her, so that she might give herself a way to cope and move on.

Now he was voicing all the doubts she had told herself over the years and turning them into weapons. The indignation and the pain sliced into her like knives. She wanted him to know the kind of helplessness he'd shown her. She wanted him to suffer.

She wanted him to be afraid. She wanted to be free of that prison in her mind, where she saw his face in every person who might love her, where she flinched at any hand that reached out to her, no matter how gentle. She wanted to know what it would be like to love herself without feeling guilt, shame and worthlessness. She wanted to experience being loved in return, without reliving every terrifying moment that taught her love didn't exist.

"Go ahead and pull the trigger, if you think you can really do it." He spread his arms wide, making himself a target. "It won't change anything."

She took a step forward, then another, until she was standing over him. She pressed the muzzle of the gun to his temple. Lia took her time, the liquor making her sluggish and shaky, and took a deep breath. When she saw his eyes widen with the realization she really was going to go through with it, she squeezed the trigger. The gun clicked against its empty chamber. "I'm not you. You might be okay with leaving my sister without one of her parents, but I'm not. I won't do that to her, not like this, not out of revenge. I think you're scared of Lucy living a life without you in it, but what are you really adding to it right now? A life fueled with violence and anger, showing her that all of her problems can be solved with someone else's suffering? You're seriously damaged if you think I'll stand by and watch this time. I won't let her be another victim like Mom, or else another mirror for you to try and mold, like me. If you ever try to threaten either of us again, I promise you that next time this gun won't be empty."

Lia's stomach rolled violently. She was out of time. She sprinted out of the room and made sure to slam the door behind her. The bathroom was only a few doors away but as the nausea crawled up the back of her throat, it might as well have been a few miles.

She made it to the toilet just in time. Feeling her way to it in the darkness and leaning over, she purged herself of the poison she had filled herself with so she might finally be rid of the poison fed to her over time. The fire of her emotions dissipated into a fever that spread along her limbs and caused her to sweat, the chill of the tiles offering her little comfort.

When it was over, her body shook from nerves and exhaustion, both warring for control as she rinsed her mouth with water and plodded to her room. Her bed was empty again, and for once, she was thankful. The sheets were cool as she sank into them and closed her eyes. Without another thought, she slept.

CHAPTER
EIGHT

LIA'S HEAD ACHED. She raised it off her pillow, and it was like a bowling ball packed with wet sand. She clawed at the edge of her mattress and dropped her leg over the edge. Her legs wobbled as she stood. She listened for any sign that Lucy or Waylen were up yet and found none. *It's too quiet.*

Lia found Waylen seated at the kitchen table with two cups of coffee set out. Had he been waiting for her? The unease in her stomach grew. "Morning."

"Where's Lucy?"

"At school. I let you sleep in."

"Why?"

"I thought you could use it. We should talk about last night." There it was again—that eerie calm. She stared at the mug on the table, not daring to sit. *Anything I say could set him off.* Then again, not doing what he expected could cause the same result. "Please, sit." His firm tone said it was a demand, not a request. Lia slipped into the chair and scooted it back. She kept her eyes on the table's surface.

"I'm not angry with you."

This was the hardest part every time. She hated when he pretended to be good, to care, when he made her doubt what her mind already knew as truth and twisted her words around. It was like it was all a game to him. A dangerous one. One that he had made her part of without ever giving her a choice. The lying game. "Okay." A neutral word choice. One that was safe. She waited for him to go on.

"I mean it. You've dealt with a lot over the past year, and I hadn't thought about how hard all of that must have been for you. So I can forgive you for acting out."

Lia fought the desire to rest her head on the table. Her eyelids drooped and her bowling ball head threatened to roll off her shoulders. She was exhausted. Not just from last night or her hangover, but a kind of spiritual exhaustion that ate away at everything good inside until all that was left were the things you didn't want to face. She thought she could put an end to that last night, but it only proved she was as trapped as ever. "Acting out?"

"You were obviously drunk and not thinking straight. I think we can both agree, it left you a little paranoid….delusional, even."

Her head shot up, and she stared at him open mouthed. "What are you talking about?"

"I'm talking about these stories you've made up in your head about me. I guess you want to cast me as a villain in your little fantasies, and that's fine. I don't know what I've ever done to deserve it, but I can deal with that."

"You don't know what you've done to deserve it? You hurt Mom! You made me watch, and when she threatened to leave, you'd use me against her. I was something she could've loved more than you, and you've always hated me for it."

"See, this is exactly what I'm talking about. Lia, if I hated you, why would I let you live here?"

"I—because you needed someone here to help take care of Lucy."

"I could have hired someone to do that. The truth is, you were in bad shape after your mom got hurt, and you didn't have any place else to go. I let you stay here because I *love* you and I don't want to see anything bad happen to you."

"That's a lie! I would've been fine on my own."

"Lia, you couldn't even handle school. You dropped out."

"I *left* to take care of Lucy!"

"Wow. I don't think it's fair to use your sister as an excuse."

"I'm not. Someone had to take care of her, and you weren't here. I got a job and everything."

"Do you really think you would've gotten that job if your best friend's dad wasn't the owner? Think about it; you have no qualifications. You have no experience. You've never really done anything with your life. It's all been handed to you."

"That's not true!" Yet, doubt slithered into the back of her brain. *He has a point. I've never held any other job but the one at Overboard. How would I know if I could've found a job anywhere else? Maybe I wouldn't have.* Her eyes filled with fresh tears.

"I'm not saying this to hurt you. I just want you to realize I'm not the bad guy here. You made these decisions on your own."

"You are. You're a horrible person."

"If I'm so horrible, then why are you staying here?"

"You hit me," she shouted.

"I lost my temper, but I don't think you can blame me for that. You've been disrespecting me ever since you moved back in. You brought it on yourself."

Lia startled at a loud knock on the door. The throb in her head intensified. Lia groaned. *I'm going to kill whoever that is.* Waylen opened the door. "Good morning, sir." A male voice. "We're going to need you and the rest of your household to come with us."

Lia went to the kitchen window to get a better look. There were no police cars out there so what….Her breath caught in her throat. There was a familiar black van parked in front of the house. *It can't be the same one, can it?* Lia sat her cup of coffee in the sink and crept into the utility room. She left the door open a crack so she could still hear.

"Who are you?"

"We're employees of LCMB. The mayor is asking that everyone come to an emergency meeting downtown."

"What for?"

"Our employer will explain everything once you get there."

"I'm not interested. Sorry." Waylen moved to close the door and one of the men kicked against it. Waylen fell backward, and they picked up his legs and dragged him across the floor. He let out a vicious roar as he grasped the door frame. Lia moved to help him, but then stopped. *If they see me, they'll try to take me, too.* Waylen looked back, and their gazes locked. The look in his eyes silently pleaded with her. She shook her head. She'd already seen what they were capable of. She carefully shut the door and looked around for a place to hide. The furnace took up most of the room and the other options were the washer and dryer. Lia was small enough to fit, but the doors had clear windows that would give her away immediately. So instead, she cowered in a corner and prayed they wouldn't check this room.

I'm so screwed. Lia couldn't hear anything outside. Every minute she sat crouched in the corner, her anxiety increased. Her stomach rumbled, and she winced. Even that sounded too loud in the enclosed space. She wished she had a watch or some indicator of how many minutes were passing. She counted Mississippis in her head. *They were so vague about why they were here. An emergency meeting?* But the more she thought about it, the more it started to make sense. An emergency meeting would accomplish one thing: bringing everyone in town together. *They're starting containment. I need to get hold of Nick.*

The last time they spoke, he had given Lia his cell phone number and told her to call him with her decision. The only problem was that her cell phone was on her nightstand. All the way in her bedroom. Lia crept around the edge of the door, staying low so anyone who might be trying to look inside the kitchen window couldn't see her. She still couldn't believe what had happened. They had taken Waylen, and they hadn't given him a choice. The front door was wide open. She knew that going to her room would leave her exposed, but she wouldn't make it very far with nothing. She had to try.

The soles of her feet squeaked against the floor as she sped into her room, shutting her door behind her. The adrenaline intensified the throbbing in her head, and the idea of collapsing on her bed and sleeping off the pain was tempting. Her hands shook as she punched in the numbers. It took her three tries before the call would go through. Blood pulsed loudly in her ears, and her breathing became shallower with each ring. *Please, pick up. Please, pick up.* "Hello?"

A feminine voice…Lia's heart sank. She was about to hang up when she a thought struck her. "Shiner?"

"Yeah?"

Lia let out a nervous giggle. "It's Lia."

"Are you okay? Why are you whispering?"

"They're starting containment. Two guys c—came and took my step-dad. They said something about an emergency meeting downtown."

"Where are you?"

"In my room. I hid, but then I realized I needed to call you. I'm scared they're coming back."

"Lia, listen to me. Nick is on his way to you. Lock your door and don't open it for anyone but him. Pack whatever you think you'll miss, okay?"

"Can you stay on the line with me until he gets here?" Lia hated how scared she sounded. Her voice was squeaky, and she was tongue-tied and tripping over her words. She had been afraid before, but that was familiar fear with a known threat. The idea of a stranger moving through her house at any minute, looking for her, made her lungs seize up and her body go cold.

"Sure. Just keep talking to me."

Lia changed her clothes and then grabbed a tote bag and filled it. She realized she didn't know Shiner or Nick any more than the men who had come to her house this morning, and yet, here she was depending on them completely. "How did you meet Nick?"

"That's a long story."

"Please? I need something else to think about."

Silence. Had the call been dropped? "The place where I lived was used in an experiment, like here. Nick showed up looking for evidence and found me. I didn't want to die so when he offered, I left with him instead."

"What happened after that?"

"What do you mean?"

"What happened to your town? To the people who lived there?"

"I don't know."

"Didn't you go back?"

"I don't see the point in going back. There wasn't much there for me to begin with."

Disbelief coursed through Lia. "Don't you care about what happened to the people there? To your family?"

"I care about me. I can't worry about them." This time it was Lia's turn to be silent. "Oh joy. I can just feel the judgment from all the way over here."

"I can't believe you don't care about your family. About

your neighbors."

"I didn't say I didn't care. I said I can't worry about them. There's a difference."

It sounds the same to me. "Then how come you stayed with Nick? You could've gone anywhere."

"I want to find the cure."

"Why?"

"Because I'm infected."

Lia stopped packing and leaned against her dresser. "You're infected?"

"Yup. This super-fun virus? It's making me blind."

Lia didn't know what to say. "I'm sorry."

"Hey, it's eat or be eaten. We all end up as Snack Packs eventually."

Lia couldn't understand how she could be so flippant. About everything. But then again, she didn't know Shiner. Maybe underneath it, she really was scared. Moving to her nightstand, Lia cleared her dresser of photos and mementos. She didn't want to lose them if they weren't able to return. Lia clasped a necklace around her neck. The charm was shaped like a key and on it were the words: *God never shuts one door without opening another.* It was one of her favorite gifts from her mom. Sighing, she slipped on her shoes. *Okay, I'm ready.*

"Let's talk about you," said Shiner.

"What about me?"

"Have you always lived in Black Ridge Falls?"

"No, we moved here when I was six."

"Where did you live before that?"

"California."

"So why'd you move here?"

"My dad died, and my mom's from here. She wanted to be around her dad, my grandpa."

"I guess that makes sense."

Lia heard a floorboard creak outside her door and she froze. She cupped her hand around the cell phone. "Someone's here."

"It's probably Nick. Just wait."

Searching for something to use as a weapon, Lia picked up the closest thing she could find. The doorknob slowly turned left and then right again. Lia tensed, raising her arm. Watching the doorknob move again, fear spread from the top of her head to her feet, her muscles clenching so tightly that her calves cramped.

The door whooshed open and Lia threw the object clutched

in her hand. The paperback thudded against the wall, soaring over the head of the man standing there. Another man slumped over face down on to the floor.

Nick smirked. "A paperback, really?"

Lia frowned at him. "It was the only thing I had close by."

"I gave you a gun." *The gun. What happened to the gun?* Lia couldn't recall whether it was with her when she ran to the bathroom. *I must have left on Waylen's floor. What would he do with it?* Unease tightened her stomach, She didn't think that Nick would like the idea that less than twenty-fours after he gave it to her, she had pointed it at her step-dad, even if it wasn't loaded.

"I didn't want to use it. What if I had accidentally shot you?"

He shrugged. "It wouldn't be my first time, but I see your point."

I wonder what he meant by that? "Who's your friend?" The other man was dressed similarly to Nick. He wore dark blue jeans with a tight fitted tee under a leather jacket. He had a skullcap on his head and thick soled boots. There were gloves on his heads.

"My guess is he was here for you. I snuck up on him as he was picking the lock."

"Why didn't he just break the door down?" *Although I'm*

really glad he didn't. I probably would've had a heart attack and died on the spot.

"Maybe he was hoping to surprise you? Maybe he was just checking to see if anyone else was home. Either way, we shouldn't stick around."

"I still need to pack Lucy's stuff."

Nick threw his hands in the air. "Why didn't you do that before I got here?"

"I was terrified for my life, that's why!" The man at Nick's feet moaned softly. She widened her eyes in panic.

Neck held out a hand to her. "We can buy her new things. C'mon."

Taking Nick's hand in hers, Lia carefully stepped over the man's body. She kicked him lightly in the side as she did. *That's for trying to kidnap me.*

Lia bent down and added the paperback to her tote bag. Nick was almost to the front door already and even though she knew they needed to hurry, Lia couldn't help but linger in the place where she grew up. All the bad couldn't erase the good, and despite everything this is where she grew up. Running her hands over the discolored patches on the wall, she wished that she could take those photos with her. *It's weird that I didn't feel this nostalgic when I left for college. Maybe part of me knew I would end up back here.* It was a sad and sobering thought. Was she ready to move on?

"Speaking of your sister, where is she? We need to pick her up before we go to get Shiner."

Lia was still lost in her thoughts. Her voice was soft and faraway. "At school."

"Oh, shit."

Lia looked over at him. Warning bells were going off inside her head like a fire truck siren. "What is it?"

"I passed the elementary school on the way here. People were evacuating it."

GETTING INTO A school during an evacuation was harder than Lia thought. A group of angry parents swarmed the front of the building. "I understand your frustration," said the principal. "However, there are concerns that the children may have been exposed to something toxic and as a precaution we're transporting all of them to Black Ridge General. You can meet the buses there if you leave now."

Lia shared a look with Nick. If they were handling the kids the same way they were handling the people who were getting sick, none of the parents would see them for a long time. As the principal walked back into the building, Nick climbed the steps after him. Lia followed closely behind. "Uh, excuse me. I still have a question."

What is he doing? He slid his eyes towards her and gave her a small shove. She frowned at him. *What? Oh.* Nick was trying to keep him busy. She looked around covertly to make sure no one else was watching and slipped past them.

The school walls were decorated with art projects and motivational posters. She walked slowly, like she belonged there. A run would only attract attention. *Stay calm. Focus on what you're here to do.* Lia had come up to the school before and luckily she knew where Lucy's classroom was. She found the locker with her sister's name tag on it and took her backpack. When she shut it, she noticed someone coming towards her in her peripheral vision. She turned and walked into the classroom.

All the kids were lined up in two rows facing the doorway. The teacher was on the phone at her desk. Lia spotted Lucy and waved to her to get her sister's attention. "Hi, Lucy's sister!" One of the other kids shouted. Lia froze, caught. *Kids. So cute. So much trouble.*

The teacher looked up and put hand over the receiver. "How did you get in here? You're not supposed to be in here right now."

Lia ignored her and held out her hand to her sister. "Lucy, come on. It's time to go."

Her sister yelled a quick goodbye to her friends and ran toward Lia. "Lucy, stop," the teacher said. Her sister stopped. "I don't know how you got in here, Miss Thomas, but Lucy is going with the other kids to the hospital. You cannot take her right now."

Lia squared her shoulders and fixed the woman with a stare. "Lucy, come here."

The little sister worried her lip and looked back and forth between the two women. She ran to Lia's side. As they walked down the hallway, Lia could hear the teacher resume her phone call. Maybe the teacher didn't have the power to stop her, but that didn't mean she wouldn't call someone that did. She slipped

Lucy's backpack onto her shoulders and reached for her. "Hold on tight, Buggy."

She could see the door at the end of the hallway. *Please let Nick still be there.* Even if someone wanted to stop them, they could easily get lost in the sea of parents outside. The combined weight of the backpack and her little sister were making it harder to run. *Almost there. Just a little bit farther.* The sound of heavy footsteps came from behind her. She huffed from the effort, and pushed herself to go faster. Someone stepped out of the shadows in front of them.

"Stop. Right now." The man in front of her didn't look like a school security guard. He looked more like the man that had tried to get to her at the house. He had gun pointed at Lia's forehead. She slowed, clutching her sister protectively. *Would they really shoot at a woman with a child? In a school?* Her eyes darted around wildly, looking for another way out. Lia glanced over her shoulder and found two more men standing behind her with their weapons trained on her back. *Stall. Think of something.* Her heart pounded and she could feel a bout of hysterical laughter coming on.

"Put the child down and walk away," the one in front of her said.

"I'm not leaving here without my sister."

She took a few steps forward and she heard the soft click of a bullet entering the chamber. *How's this for irony?* She paused again. *How am going to get out of this?* Her stomach tightened again. The gun was aimed at her and not her sister, so they wanted to keep the children alive. What worried her was what would happen to them once they got to the hospital.

"Let go of the child and we won't shoot you."

Her sister started to cry. She needed to figure a way out of this, fast. "You're saying the kids have been exposed to something toxic." The man nodded once, all business. "What about the teachers? They've been around the kids all day. If the kids were exposed to something than they were, too. Everyone who comes into contact with them would be."

"What's your point?"

"I'm unarmed. I'm not a threat. But I have been in contact with the kids. Let me go on the bus and ride to the hospital with you."

He thought about that for a few minutes. He lowered his weapon. "Fine. We're loading through that exit. You'll go first."

Lia nearly collapsed from nerves. "Okay."

"Wait." The man marched up to her. "Hold out your arms

and spread your feet."

Lia did as she was told and he quickly padded her down. She felt his hand reach for her cell phone in her back pocket. "She's clear!"

"What about my phone?"

"Move." She turned around and followed the other two men down another hallway in the opposite direction. When they got to the door, one of them banged on it twice and it opened from the outside. They stepped through and Lia felt the muzzle of a gun press against her back. "Get going," he hissed in her ear. Her breaths shortened into gasps and prayed she didn't cry. *He's probably the one in charge.* A white plastic tarp was sealed around the doorway creating a tunnel which most likely lead all the way to the bus. Lia felt the muzzle press into her back again. She walked.

Nick won't know where I've gone. What if he tried to leave without us? The exit setup made Lia believe that there may be some truth to the toxin story, after all. If there were, was it the water borne virus or something else? Her insides twisted at the thought of Lucy being sick. Tears were still soaking into the fabric of Lia's t-shirt and she made shushing noises to try and comfort her. "You're okay, buggy."

Even the bus was covered in a white sheet. The only part that wasn't covered was the windshield. The driver was wearing a yellow hazmat suit and didn't look up as they boarded. Lia scooted into one of the bus seats. Lucy sat next to her. The man who threatened Lia slid in at the end. Her sister buried her face in Lia's side and Lia wrapped an arm around her. The man winked at Lia.

"Everybody comfortable?" The man kept his eyes forward but Lia could see that he was smiling a little. He laid his gun across his lap, the treat clear.

Lia bore holes into the side of his head, but he didn't move. "Why are you doing this?"

"Because I care about the health and well-being of children."

The other children boarded the bus. They stared wide-eyed at the covered windows. More armed men walked in behind them and lead them to their seats. Most of them looked at Lia with wide eyes, as if they were surprised to see her there. When the last one took his seat at the back of the bus the doors shut with a snap. The breaks hissed as they pulled away. With each bump they hit, Lia tensed. They were getting farther and farther from the school. *What if I can't keep her safe?* She looked around at the dozens of other children on the bus. *What's going to happen to them if we can't find a cure in time?* Lia already knew the answer. If everything Nick and Shiner said were true and they couldn't find a cure, every one of these children were going to die.

CHAPTER NINE

ONCE THEY REACHED the hospital, everyone was lead off the bus in groups. Their group (which included Lia, Lucy and twelve other children) was the last to go. The man seated next to them made Lia and Lucy walk up front with him while another man hovered near the end. When they stepped through the sliding doors of the lobby, she tried to make eye contact with the receptionist, but the woman never looked up. They forced everyone into the elevators and pushed the button to the basement. Lia's throat went dry. *What are they keeping down there?*

The answer as it turned out, was people. They stepped off the elevator and Lia was shocked to see close to a hundred people crammed into the hallway. The walls were standard gray cinder block and the overhead florescent lights flickered with a loud bug zapper like noise. There were women in white lab coats moving through the crowd and writing notes on clipboards. One approached her and she drew Lucy closer to her side. "Can I have your names, please?"

"That depends on what it's for."

"Were you not at the emergency meeting this morning?"

"No, I wasn't."

The woman sighed. "Everyone here is being vaccinated against or treated for an immune system threatening toxin that's leaked into Black Ridge Fall's water supply. The vaccine has minimal side effects and is mandatory. No exceptions." The way she said it made Lia think that she had repeated it many times already. "Now, I need your names so I can check you off the list of residents that we still need to round up."

This doesn't make any sense. If the supply is already contaminated with the virus, and this is something they want, then why would they be giving people vaccines against it? No matter how mandatory it is, I doubt anything "good" for us would cause them to pull people out of their homes by force. She wasn't sure whether to lie or tell the truth, and the woman gave no indication that she wouldn't wait there all day, if necessary. "Do you have any more information on the vaccine, like a pamphlet or brochure I could look at?"

It was subtle, but Lia saw the woman glance at one of the hired guns who forced them onto the bus. He pushed off the wall and headed towards them. "Are we going to have a problem here?"

She smiled. "Oh no, I'm just curious. Our names are Ophelia Thomas and Lucy Lancaster."

The woman checked her clipboard and gave it two quick checks. "Thank you. I just have a couple more questions and then you can wait for your name to be called. How often would you say that the two of you drink water?"

"A lot," Lia lied.

"How many glasses would you say per day?"

"Three. I try not to give her any before bed, because you know. *Accidents.*" Lia knew she was babbling. It happened every time she got nervous. This was a lie she had been unprepared for. The woman fixed her with a humorless stare.

"And how would you characterize your health lately?"

"Okay. The heat gets to us, but nothing serious."

"Have you felt any nausea or dizziness? Had any sudden nosebleeds? Have you noticed any headaches or excessive sweating?"

Most of those symptoms were hard to fake. She decided to tell the truth. "No."

"Okay. Also, do you shower regularly?" Lia felt of jolt of panic zip through her system. *Could the virus be absorbed through the skin?* She had taken a shower this morning. *Could it already be inside of me?* Her voice sounded unsteady when she spoke again.

"Yes, we do."

"Great. Thanks. Just sit tight and when we call your name, you can proceed up the hall to the front of the line."

Lia knelt down next to Lucy. "How are you doing, Ladybug?"

"I don't like it here. I want to go home."

"We will." Lia looked around for any other exits. There were men guarding the elevator so they couldn't go back up the way they came. "We're going to go home real soon."

Lucy began to cry again. This time it sounded more like a tantrum than fear. *I wish I had my cell phone. I wonder if Nick or Shiner know what's going on? We can't have been gone that long.* She pressed the heels of her palms to her eyes. When she opened them again, Lia spied movement out of the corner of her eye. It looked like the shadows were moving. *Okay, now I really am losing it.* That's when she saw it. The light reflected off a coat of ebony fur and a pair of big yellow eyes. *They're keeping wild animals down here?* That didn't make sense.

She waved her arms until she had a guard's attention. "What's down the other end of this hallway?"

He raised an eyebrow. "Just the bathrooms."

"Do you mind if I take her? I don't think she's gone since this morning."

"I'll have to escort you. You aren't allowed to go on your own."

The lights only worked every other minute down there. More than once, she had to stop because Lucy wouldn't go any farther in the dark. Even after all that the guard never left them behind. Lia listened close for any sounds that might be from a wild animal, but she heard none. When they reached the door to the bathroom, he held the door open and walked inside after them. "I don't think so. She's a little girl."

"My orders are clear. I'm not to leave the residents alone for any amount of time."

"Stand outside the door! You can obviously see there's no

way to get out of here." Which was true. The bathroom he brought them to was tiny, with only one toilet and sink. It didn't even have any windows.

"Five minutes. Then I'm coming in." Lia shot him the finger on his way out.

They were drying off their hands when they heard the guard scream. Lia stopped, listening hard, until the scratching started. It reminded her of the way a pet scratched at the door to be let in. *Scratch, scratch, scratch. Pause. Scratch, scratch, scratch. Pause.* Lia's heart was pounding. She waited a few minutes until the scratching stopped again, and carefully turned the knob. The guard was lying on the floor in front of the door. He wasn't hurt or bleeding, and by the rise and fall of his chest, Lia could see he was still breathing. Sitting across the hall was a black jaguar. Lia could almost swear it was the same one that had wandered into her bedroom. As she tiptoed slowly out of the bathroom with Lucy in her arms, it raised its head like it had been waiting for them.

Lia stilled, and watched as it moved again. It crossed the hall to the door next to theirs and started pawing at it. It sat down on the floor and looked up at her expectantly. When she didn't move, it pawed at the door again. Finally, Lia moved the other door. It stood up and watched her. *I really hope there's not another one locked in here.* She pushed in the door and the jaguar disappeared inside. Lia breathed a sigh of relief. But then it was there again, peeking around the door frame. "Follow the kitty!" yelled Lucy and Lia shushed her. Except the cat seemed to nod its head, like it agreed.

What are you, the jungle cat whisperer? Lia rolled her eyes and started walking back to the elevators. The cat let out a low grumble from behind her. She turned, and it threw its head back. If she *was* a jungle cat whisperer, she was sure it'd was saying, "*c'mon already.*"

Lia didn't see it until she was three steps into the other bathroom. There was a faint light shining through a hole in the bathroom wall plaster. Her heart skipped a beat. *They could get out of here! They could find Nick!* The jaguar's mouth dropped open, resembling a smile. Someone shouted and the sound was getting closer and closer to where they were. "Can you get him on the radio?" She heard someone say. *They're looking for us.*

The jaguar's growl wasn't friendly this time. It snarled, its ears flattening on its head. It placed itself between them and the doorway. Lia shut it so that they were hidden a bit longer. Her heart hammered unevenly. "Lucy, stay quiet, okay? I'm going to get us out of here." Her sister nodded, pressing an index finger to her lips.

The opening in the plaster was tiny and there was no way Lia could squeeze through. She punched the wall experimentally and the skin split on her knuckles. She winced and rubbed her hand. The noise attracted the jaguar's attention, who turned and cocked its head to the side. "The opening's too small," she explained. "It needs to be bigger."

And now I've become the BeastMaster. Wonderful.

The jaguar growled. Lia back up a few paces and so did it. Without warning, it launched itself at the wall and started clawing at the opening. Within seconds bits of wallpaper and plaster cover the floor. The hole was big enough for her to crawl through. The jaguar looked at her.

"Um, thanks. Thank you."

It gave a tiny grunt. Lia took that to mean "you're welcome."

LIA DIDN'T WANT to take any chances to see what would happen if they stayed. Still, she had no cell phone, no vehicle and all of the stuff she was packed was sitting in Nick's van. *I would try going back home, but that's probably the first place they'll look when they find out we're gone.* Guilt gnawed at her over not being able to pack Lucy's things. The things Lia kept packed in her backpack wasn't going to cut it. Nick said they could buy Lucy new things, but she didn't have that much money to begin with. Suddenly, she remembered. Lia had asked Nicole Cates to keep some of their stuff in her car! She still had the problem of tracking down Nicole, but it was better than nothing. *The only question left is how to get wherever we're going.*

The jaguar was pacing in circles. Lia watched it as it moved back and forth along the side of the building. "What's with you?"

It took off running. Lia grabbed Lucy's hand and they struggled to keep up. She figured if they could keep it in eyesight that would be good enough. She watched as it stopped and looked back at them. *It better not be chasing an ice cream truck or something.* Panting, Lia bent over and tried to catch her breath. When she looked up, it was doing one of those open-mouthed grins again. Somehow, it lead them straight to Nick's van. Lia gazed at the jungle cat in amazement. *Okay, so not only am I talking to animals, I'm also somehow sending telepathic signals to them. Unless…* Cats could pick up scents just like dogs, so why not jungle cats? "Is that why you've been following me? Because I smell like Nick or Shiner?"

The jaguar didn't answer. Or at least it didn't answer like it did before. *I've not only lost it, but I've fully invested in my delusion.* Thinking of delusions brought back Waylen's words from this morning. *Had that only been this morning? Was he one of the people in that basement?* None of them looked like they were under duress, but if Waylen had been there, he wouldn't have been quiet about it. *Why would Nick be here? Was it to find me?* But how would he know where she was?

It's because E.J.'s here. He's leaving me behind. She didn't expect the realization to sting, but it did. She trusted Nick against her better judgment and the betrayal left bitterness in its wake. The worst part about it was that she didn't blame Nick at all. She blamed herself. *This is what I get for being so stupid.* She kicked one of tires out of spite. It didn't do anything, but she felt a little better.

A sound like a canon went off somewhere close by. Lia dropped fat on her stomach, covering Lucy's body with her own.

There were footsteps coming towards them. They crunched across the asphalt of the parking lot, sounding hurried. "Lia!"

She looked up and saw Nick sprinting towards her. "Get in the van," he called. *The van's open?* Rising up on her elbows, she saw that Shiner was with him, too. They were pushing something on a gurney. Behind them were a dozen armed guards.

"Crap." She stood up and slid open the side of the van. She lifted Lucy up and climbed in after her. Crawling to the driver's seat, she was dismayed to see that the keys weren't anywhere to be found. She turned around and placed Lucy in the passenger seat. At least it had a seatbelt. Hearing a whimpering sound, Lia looked back. The jaguar was watching them with pleading eyes. "Oh, you've *got* to be kidding me." She sighed. "Get in then." It leapt inside and curled up in the corner. Nick climbed into the back seconds later. He grabbed hold of the gurney while Shiner pushed it inside from the other end. When it was in place she hopped in and slammed the door shut. Lia moved as he stepped over her to start the engine.

The van came to life with a roar that almost drowned out Shiner's yell of surprise. "What the hell is *that* doing in here?"

"It's a long story. She's really tame."

"For a wild animal! Nick, tell her she's crazy."

"We don't have time to argue," he said. "Hold on."

NICK DROVE BACK to the Seabreeze motel. Nick's driving made her nauseous and Lia was glad when they stopped. Shiner kept her eyes on the jaguar as she got out. Nick walked around to the back and froze. The jaguar stood up and whined. It was a sad sound. "It's not possible," Nick whispered.

Shiner stood with a hand on her hip. "I know, Lia's crazy. It's always the quiet ones you have to watch out for."

Lia watched the emotions flickering across Nick's face and recognized something like longing or anguish. She looked at the jaguar and could swear that the same things were mirrored in its eyes. *It's almost like he's seen it before.* A thought struck her. "Nick, is this a person? Do you know her?"

Shiner's mouth dropped open. "No way! That's not possible, right?" Shiner looked at Nick for confirmation.

Nick was still staring at the jaguar. "Her name is Sabrina."

The silence that followed was heavy with disbelief. Shiner was the first to break it. "Let's be honest, animals are a lot harder to tell apart than people. How can you be sure that's even her? That could be anyone. That could be a real jaguar!"

Nick shook his head. "It's her. I know it."

Shiner opened her mouth then closed it again. "We don't have time to argue, right? Those guys could track us down at any time."

Lia turned towards them as she unbuckled Lucy's seatbelt. "About that, why were they chasing you? What's in there?" The container strapped to the stretcher was rectangular and covered in a blue sheet. Wires snaked out of it, attaching to some type of remote that beeped occasionally. It reminded Lia of the machine that monitored people's vitals.

Shiner and Nick exchanged a look. Shiner answered in a quiet, reserved voice. "E.J."

She crept towards the box, kneeling down to touch it. It reminded her of her mom's coffin. *No, E.J. isn't dead. He can't be dead.* But there was no oxygen tank, and how could he survive without oxygen? She felt lightheaded. "Open it," she demanded. "I want to see that it's him."

Nick shook his head. "I don't think that's—"

"I don't give a damn what you think! Open it. Now."

Nick sighed. Taking a set of keys out of his pocket, he went and unlocked the door to the room. When he walked out again there was a box cutter in his hand. He climbed into the van and unbuckled the straps first. They fell away with a loud clunk. He then cut a slit along the top. He grasped the two flaps and yanked them down so that the top was fully visible. Lia gasped.

The container was made of glass. Inside, E.J. was submerged in some kind liquid. His body floated, gently rocking back and forth and bumping the edges. He was naked. His eyes were closed and his dark hair danced like a jellyfish around his face. Tiny bubbles streamed from his closed lips. Nick rapped quickly on the glass. E.J.'s eyes flew open.

Lia jumped back. *How is that possible? How is he breathing?* Then she remembered the tiny slits that formed on the side of his neck. Lia put her face to the glass and squinted. It was almost imperceptible, but she could see bubbles streaming from there, too. E.J. was breathing underwater. Her heart sank. *Does this mean that we're too late?*

E.J. turned his head and met her eyes. *Lia.* He mouthed the word and a large bubble floated to the surface. "I'm here," She said, her voice cracking. Tears streamed down her cheeks. E.J. pressed his palm to the glass. Lia swallowed thickly and placed her own against it. He spoke again. *What's happening to me?*

Lia rubbed her eyes with the back of her hand and sniffed. "It's going to be okay. We're going to fix it." She spoke loudly and slowly, wondering if he could hear her under the glass.

Nick nudged her shoulder and handed her a tissue. Lia gently wiped her eyes and nose. "We *can* fix it right? We can make him human again?" Lia chest ached. It felt like her heart was breaking. "Please, fix it."

It was suddenly all too real. Mrs. Ryan. Anita. E.J. All those kids. So many lives were going to be lost if they didn't do something. Lia would lose one of the only people she trusted. Eddie would lose his only son. The feeling in her chest grew tighter and she tried to draw in deep breaths. No matter what she did, the feeling only increased. She opened her mouth wider but it was like her chest wouldn't rise, like there were tight bands holding it in place. Tears pricked at the corner of her eyes as the light around her grew fuzzy.

"Lean forward," Nick commanded, placing a hand on her back. "Deep breaths. In. Out. Slowly."

Lia did as he said, until the bands around her chest loosened. Soon she was breathing normally again. "We're going to try." Nick replied. "We're going to do everything we can. But it's not going to be easy. I'm going to do what I can to keep everyone safe, but it will be dangerous at times. People are going to come after us. I need to know that you're prepared for that. I need to know that you'll trust me and trust my judgment."

Trust wasn't easy for Lia. She always lived with her back to an exit, ready to escape before anything became too complicated or difficult. She never wanted to end up trapped like her mom. She needed to know everything about a situation beforehand so that there was never a chance that she could get hurt. Traveling with Nick didn't guarantee anything. She would be facing the world blind, making decision based on her instincts. Not facts. She wouldn't be responsible for just herself, either. Her decisions would affect Lucy, too.

When she didn't answer, Nick shoved his hands in his pockets and stood up. "We're going to spend the night here. We need to pack and decide the best way to get around the roadblocks. You and Lucy can sleep in the front room. In the morning, you can make your decision."

"There are roadblocks?"

Shiner nodded. "Quarantine's in full effect. No one gets in. No one gets out."

ACKNOWLEDGEMENTS

This book wouldn't exist without the love and support of so many people. Thank you all. I'd fill up a thousand pages to thank you all individually if I could. Please know that I see you.

A huge thank you to Dionne Lister! Without your hard work and dedication, this book would *not* read as well as it does. Any mistakes are my own. (It's probably the feelings. I've given up character feelings for Lent.) I'm still learning, but you make me a better writer. I'm looking forward to working on the rest of the book with you.

Najla Qamber, thank you SO MUCH for this spectacular cover! This book was worth breaking into parts just for it alone. You're magic.

Nadège Richards, thank you again for what I'm sure will be *incredible* interior design work. (I haven't seen it yet, but I know it will be flawless.)

To Papa, who sacrificed so much during this process. You

never gave up on the idea that I would figure this out. Thank you (again) for putting up with me, my late nights/early morning, all my "weird" tendencies and for loving me through everything. I love you. Long live King Bob!

To Mom, I'm scared for you to read this. It will probably be difficult for you to read, but don't worry. It gets better. I love you and thank you.

To Cooper, hearing your little brother ask about your books and knowing he wants to read them is the second best feeling in the world. The first is hearing him say "I love you." You're really cool, and I feel lucky everyday that I get to be your big sister. Thank you for the support. I love you always.

To Aunt Kelly, who is always my number one fan. Where would I be without your support? Nowhere. You're amazing and worthy of so much. Remember that. I love you and thank you.

Ginger, here's part of the book? (Please, don't throw things at me. Just kidding, but seriously.) Look, jaguar on the cover! I will deliver more **pages** soon. You more than anyone have pushed for this book to get done and I hope this start does you proud. Love ya, Girlie! (P.S. I think I've become Shigure.)

Carol, the realization that you have to wait for the next two parts of this book is probably going to make you as upset as the fact that I never finished COTN. (I will finish this one, promise.) I hope you enjoy the start. Thank you for all your support! I'm grateful that you're my friend.

Elyse, hooray team! I don't know where that came from. I'm *tired.* We've both worked very hard these past few weeks and I look forward to finally being able to see you again. Let's have cupcakes. We've earned it. Thanks for believing in me! Love you.

Eli, welcome to my dark little corner of the world. I take comfort in knowing that you can **never** leave. (Just kidding? I blame sleep deprivation.) Seriously, thank you so much. Your words may seem miniscule to you, but you contribute so much to my life and my work. Love you.

Ashley F. (Phillip-Ashley), you're awesome. Believe it. Thank you for encouraging me and always being there to talk. I hope that I add something good to your life, however small. I can't wait until you're published.

Ashley (mi hermana, my love), I hope you like this story. You've been in my life for such a long time and I can still remember the first time you read something of mine. (Did I just rhyme? I think I did.) I hope my books always get that reaction from you. That's how I know I'm doing a good job. I love you (and I miss you) so much!

Abby, look what I wrote! I hope you like it. I hope it inspires you to write. Thank you for your support. I love you, hermana. I want to see your face. Let's work on that.

Steven, I had to put you in here. You know why? Because you keep calling me J.K. Rowling and now my book is so large that I have to break it into parts. I blame you (and procrastination.) Thanks for believing that I'll be on her level someday. It means everything. It really does.

To Colleen Gleason, the best author out there. I've already said a lot when it comes to you. Your support means everything. I hope that this book surprises you and that you like it. Thank you for reading. (Michigan authors still rock!)

Lastly, thank you to all of the readers who will pick up this book. I hope you enjoyed it. (Don't be too mad about the cliffhanger. Parts two and three are coming soon.) If you like this book (and even if you didn't) please think about leaving a review. Reviews are helpful to authors.

ABOUT THE AUTHOR

N.J. Ember is a paranormal fiction author who loves to write stories about survival and triumph over adversity. Whether her characters are dealing with the paranormal or everyday life, she seeks to show that strength is not always about being superhuman or invulnerable. She enjoys anything with mystery, suspense and horror, so when she's not writing you can find her watching shows like Orphan Black, Penny Dreadful and Sherlock. She currently lives in Michigan with her grandpa and a forever growing collection of books and Funko Pop! figures.

Website: www.njember.com/
Newsletter: http://eepurl.com/ZP9iX
Facebook: www.facebook.com/njember.author
Twitter: www.twitter.com/nj_ember
Instagram: www.instagram.com/njember.author/

ISOLATION

by N.J. Ember

They used to prey on us. Now we poison them.

After spending the summer visiting her father in the
Philippines, seventeen year old Analyn Santos was hoping for a
fresh start back home in the States. What she hadn't counted
on was being abducted from the airport.

Why would they take her? Ransom money? No matter
what she tries to bargain with, her captors only seem
to want one thing: her blood. Lots of it.

Desperate to survive, Analyn bides her time until she can make
her escape; only something seems to be moving out there in the
darkness. Suddenly, she isn't so sure that the only threat lies
within the derelict house…or how long it will be before
whatever it is finds a way inside.

Coming soon…